Evan Wechman is a freelance journalist who has reported on both political and cultural issues occurring in society. He is also a professional speaker who addresses obsessive-compulsive disorder and other mental health issues to help erase the stigma of living with a mental illness. Evan grew up suffering in silence from the damaging effects of OCD but has learned how to fight back.

I dedicate this book to my entire family, especially my parents, who always provided the love I needed.

Evan Wechman

FAMILY ILLNESS

AUSTIN MACAULEY PUBLISHERS™
LONDON • CAMBRIDGE • NEW YORK • SHARJAH

Ordering Information
Quantity sales: Special discounts are available on quantity purchases by corporations, associations, and others. For details, contact the publisher at the address below.

Publisher's Cataloging-in-Publication data
Wechman, Evan
Family Illness

ISBN 9781647503482 (Paperback)
ISBN 9781647503475 (Hardback)
ISBN 9781647503499 (ePub e-book)

Library of Congress Control Number: 2021906251

www.austinmacauley.com/us

First Published (2021)
Austin Macauley Publishers LLC
40 Wall Street, 33rd Floor, Suite 3302
New York, NY 10005
USA

mail-usa@austinmacauley.com
+1 (646) 5125767

I got out of bed and left my room where the other patients were still sleeping. It was the middle of the night but no matter how much medicine the doctors gave me, I could not sleep. I was too preoccupied with these racing thoughts that I was having. There was no one to talk to but I knew my mind was growing frantic. None of my friends would want to hear from me and so I was left with trying to find solace from my family. Both my older and younger brothers were surely asleep, as they had real jobs to get up for in the morning. I could never be like them. Their lives were so simple and clearly defined. They were not forced to endure what I had been suffering from. They had escaped the disease and had the privilege of not knowing what I knew. Their lives were intact and mine was crumbling to pieces.

As I paced back and forth in the hallway upstairs, I tried not to make any noise that would alarm either the sickly patients or the terrible staff. I looked at the yellow phone on the wall and retreated to my usual patterns. I had to call my parents, which is what I always did when I was in trouble. I sought the aid and comfort of them, even if it killed them.

"Mom!" I yelled into the phone.

"What are you doing, calling the house so late?"

"Mom, something terrible is happening."

"What? What, Steve, are you talking about?"

"Something unforeseen and ugly is occurring."

"You're scaring me," she said.

"Mom, something wicked has come my way."

"For Christ's sake, Steve, what is going on?"

"The devil has come for me and has taken control of my mind and body."

"The devil, Steven, has not possessed you."

"How do you know that?"

"Because if you were possessed, you wouldn't be frantically calling me asking for reassurance."

"I think he has possessed me like a predator consuming his prey."

"Steve, please consider what you are saying. The devil has not possessed you. You are a kind person and as Jews, we don't believe in him."

"Mom, I'm terrified that I'm going to hurt someone like some kind of monster."

"Where is all this crap coming from?"

"Where is what crap coming from?" I repeated while my anger was intensifying.

"This shit about you, the devil, possession, and everything else that enters your mind."

"During group therapy today, someone was talking about him and it got me thinking that if I ask the devil to possess me, then he will."

"Then don't ask him!" she screamed.

"Oh, so you admit, Mom, that it is a possibility."

"I don't admit anything," she said.

I was becoming more irritated as was she. It didn't take my mother long for her to get aggravated with me. "Mom, if due to my illness, I ask the devil to possess me, will he?"

"No."

"But how do you know this for certain, Mom?"

"Because there is no devil, Steve. It's just a bunch of nonsense."

"You're saying that there is absolutely no Satan, Lucifer, or anyone else by that name who can take over my soul."

"It is not remotely possible," her voice was shaking and I could sense that she was reaching her breaking point with me, her young adult son—a complete failure.

I could hear my father grab the phone.

"Now you listen to me, Steve, and you listen good. There is no devil. Never was, never will be. So you could ask 100 times and it doesn't matter. We are Jewish and we don't believe in any of this bullshit." My father, whom I always sought for reassurance and support in my times of weakness, sounded stern.

"Dad, please help me!" I cried.

"I'm trying to, son, but please just get off the phone and go to bed."

"Dad, please listen and help me."

"It's 2 am, Steve. What do you want from me?" he sounded exasperated.

"I want to come home."

I realized then that I was barefoot, and wearing nothing but a pair of boxer shorts. If any members of the staff were to see me, I would be in big trouble. However, I had more pressing concerns at the moment. I would not let myself be worried about such trivial issues while I was in the midst of trying to save lives.

"You are not better yet. The doctors need for you to stay longer. They told us that you might try something like this."

"The doctors don't know everything, Dad. There is no cure for obsessive-compulsive disorder."

"Maybe not, but you can learn to live with it and not let it terrorize your life."

"Let me come home, Dad, and I will work on things at our house in New York. I hate it here in Ohio. It's boring and dull. I miss the excitement of New York."

"You don't even go out much, Steve, so living at home is not helping any of us."

"Dad—"

He cut me off and replied, "Steve, this is a dire situation. Please try to take stock of things and work with the staff."

My father was right. Though I was depressed also at home, I missed the smell of the great homemade meals my mother would prepare for me. After dinner, there would always be stimulating political conversations with my father, if I felt up to it. He was an ardent Republican who always taught me to stick with the political party that would support Israel. I had never been to Israel and had problems with both Judaism and Christianity so I wasn't sure why he was so passionate about his views. But, possibly there were things about my dad that didn't make sense to me and never would.

I just hoped that my dad was right in that there was no devil and we were indeed the chosen ones. Of course, as some of the patients would say, that was complete bullshit.

Though I was always proud of my culture, such conversations seemed distant, cold, and irrelevant now. The food here was terrible so I was awfully hungry during this extremely hot summer. I yearned for the comforts of watching television in my air-conditioned home but knew the quality of my life was sharply declining.

"Give it some time, Steve. There is no rush. Mom and I just want you to get better."

"But Dad, I am getting worse and Mom just wants me out of her hair."

"Your mother loves you and takes care of you."

"I'm not going to debate that, Dad. I know she loves me but she has an odd way of showing it. Besides, everyone is obsessed with morality here."

"So are you, Steve Goldberg," he said rather sarcastically. I could picture him smiling on the other end as if he caught me in a political game of gotcha.

"Yes, I know but that is absolutely why I need to get out of here. Everyone talks about God and Christianity. I am the only Jew in this disgusting hospital."

"It's not a hospital, Steve. It's just a clinic for people with a high level of OCD."

I chuckled slightly as the humor was rich in his last statement. The brochure that they mailed me last year presented itself as an educational clinic with lots of great instruction being doled out. In reality, I could now see that it was a psychiatric hospital. There were many doctors prescribing various medications, social workers espousing outdated theories, and per diem employees physically restraining patients during temper tantrums. I wished now that I never asked my mother to put me on the waiting list to be admitted. But, then again, there were a lot of things I wished I had done differently in my life. I was a young adult but I was full of sorrow and regret. Every choice I made seemed worse than the one before.

"Dad, it's a hospital and I want to go back to New York where there are other people like me."

"What do you mean?"

"Jews, Dad. I want to be amongst other Jews."

"Maybe you have been sheltered, Steve, but this is the world we live in. You are part of a minority. And again, you barely leave the house so what difference does it make. Yes, your family is Jewish and we love you but you don't talk to really anyone else so what difference does it make what religion they are?"

"Have you been listening to anything I have been saying, Dad?" I said rather condescendingly.

"Well, spell it out for me, Steve."

"I would not care if the other patients would stop preaching to me all this Bible shit. I want to put an end to my fear of going to hell."

"You are not going to hell, Mr. Goldberg. It's all in your mind."

"What if you are wrong, Dad?"

"I'm not. I'm as sure of that as anything."

There was then silence for a few seconds as I wasn't sure what to say and I sensed my dad was feeling trapped in my conversation.

As I waited for my dad to say something, I could hear my mom screaming in the background, "Bob, Bob, we have to go back to bed. This is not fair to us."

"Steve, I have to go," he whispered into the phone just loud enough so I can hear him.

This reminded me of the numerous times my mother would lose patience with me when I was at home. It also fueled inside me a lot of resentment. I was almost 30 years old and my mom showed me little respect, treating me as a mere nuisance. She loved my two brothers more than me as they were easier in all aspects of her life. Their hatred toward me caused them to flee their home state and I knew my mom resented the hell out of me.

"Dad, you didn't answer my question," I felt my voice shaking like when I was a child in Hebrew School and the teacher called on me to read the Torah which I struggled with. I struggled with that old, archaic, language which served me no real purpose in the outside world.

"What question?"

"What if the Jews are wrong?"

"There is no hell, Steve. Please, your mother is getting angry and I'm starting to feel a little weak."

However, I pressed on.

"How do you know God wouldn't punish me?"

"I can't give you all the answers."

"I need the answers now."

"Go to sleep. You will feel better in the morning."

"How can I sleep with this war going on in my head?" My voice was raised and I could feel my hands shaking. They always shook when I was nervous, which was most of the time. I didn't know if it was a side effect of one of the meds they were giving to me or my body was just weaker than others.

"Steve, I'm going to call the clinic and speak to someone if you don't get off the phone."

"Fuck you, Dad!" I shouted as I hung up the yellow phone that was full of many terrible germs from the sickos that were living here.

I couldn't believe I cursed at him. I was an angry person and though I lost my temper with my mom often, it was rare that I did so with my favorite parent, the one who always stuck by me. I felt my body fall to the floor as I sat on the ground curled up in the fetal position. I was indeed a baby, dependent on others, unable to survive on my own. I wasn't crying, though I wanted to do so.

At that point, I thought I heard some rumblings downstairs from the night staff guy but then was able to hear the television. But he didn't care about me. He probably heard me but was too busy watching the Yankees-Indians game. I thought about going downstairs to try to catch a glimpse of the game but knew my mind was too full of noise to be entertained by anything else. I felt like calling my parents again and giving them a piece of my mind, but I knew they wouldn't stand for it. They would indeed call the hospital and I didn't feel like going through another confrontation with anyone else since it would just be more trouble. They would yell at me and tell me that I wasn't dealing with my illness in the right manner. They were so strict and so I often thought of them as Nazis in their persecution of me and the other patients who were not doing well. It was all bullshit anyway, as I had seen no one be cured. Yes, there were one or two people—or consumers as the hospital liked to politically correctly identify them— who seemed happy. But they were not truly sick. They had a few symptoms of the disease but by the grace of God, as my mom often said, they had not truly been touched.

I started pacing the hallway again because I knew I wouldn't sleep. Out of fear that someone might hear me, I walked into one of the bathrooms in the corner and walked up to the sink. I splashed water on my face but knew I would not be refreshed. I started to stare at my face in the mirror and was just disgusted with myself. I was considered good looking by some women and my family always told me how beautiful I was, but I didn't see that. I saw a chubby-faced man with wrinkly skin—skin like an older man who had been fighting his whole life in war, perhaps even a concentration camp sufferer. I then spat at myself in the mirror as I hated the gross picture looking back at me.

"I hate you, Steve Goldberg. I hate you, you stupid Jew."

March 5, 1980

I was only seven, but that Saturday morning I awoke to horrible news. I was the middle child of three sons. My parents and brothers were passing around the newspaper. My younger brother—who was five years old and had not learned to read yet—was just interested in looking at the comics but my older brother, Sam, saw something that caught his eye. He was 13, an avid reader who always seemed to know everything, and passed the paper to my father.

My dad read the paper for a few moments and then firmly made an announcement. He said that Todd Stein, a councilman and father of a schoolmate of ours, had been tragically killed in a car accident the previous night in New York City. We lived in an affluent suburb about ten miles north of the city. My dad was a prominent professor at a university in Manhattan and he commuted to the city daily. Little did I know at the time, the effect that this incident would have on me. I kept thinking that if it could happen to Councilman Stein, then it could happen to my father as well. My father was an excellent driver, even during the icy snowstorms we had during the winters, but anything could happen to anyone.

My two brothers played wiffleball with each other outside in our big backyard most of Saturday and Sunday, Sam trying to teach Scott how to hit. Sam had asked me numerous times if I would like to play, but I felt like just watching the Yankees game on the television with my father. It appeared that my dad knew I was worried about something since he kept asking me if I was okay. I didn't want him to worry so I just nodded. I wasn't sure if he knew the truth. I wanted to speak to him but I felt shy and anxious.

My mother spent most of the weekend upstairs reading her books. I was kind of confused about why nobody was talking about Todd Stein. Scott was possibly too young to understand the danger of the situation. Sam though, knew Todd's son, Noah, and even though they did not hang out, I was surprised to find that Sam was not preoccupied with how Noah would be feeling. They were in the same class at school. *How could he seem so at ease?* I wondered.

On Sunday night, I went to my bedroom hoping to fall asleep but it was pointless. The incident with Mr. Stein was weighing on my mind as if I was being crushed by a big stone. I kept imagining his car being hit by another vehicle and suddenly dying. I was worried about Noah, even though he probably didn't even know who I was. How would his mother tell him that his father was dead? And if this could happen to Noah's dad, it could happen to mine, too. However, I was more concerned with my dad's well-being. Nobody in my family was scared of my strong father getting hurt, except for me. It was dominating my every thought for I couldn't imagine a world without my dad. I wandered around my bedroom a couple of times, just pacing back and forth, hoping the thoughts would go away or I would get too tired to stay awake. Nothing was working, and I feared how I would be tomorrow in school. Even though I hated school and felt shy around most of my classmates, I didn't want any attention drawn to me. I was scared my teacher would yell at me if I seemed distracted or if I started to cry. There was no way I could cry in school and not get in trouble.

I decided to walk downstairs to where my father was sitting on his favorite chair eating some potato chips. I felt somewhat reassured that he would be okay because as I stared at him, I could see how involved he was with the television show and not concerned at all about driving to work the next morning.

My father noticed me and said, "Steve, my little tiger, what are you doing down here?"

"I had a nightmare," I lied.

"What was it about?"

"I don't want to talk about it. Can I watch TV with you?"

"Maybe for about ten minutes but your mother wants you to get enough rest for school."

"Dad, I don't think I can fall asleep tonight."

"Give it ten minutes, Stevie, and then I will help you go to bed."

"Thanks, Dad."

After about 20 minutes, my father reminded me that it was time to go back upstairs to sleep.

We went to my bedroom and he tucked me in and shut off the lights.

"Give yourself a chance to fall asleep," he said.

"I don't think I can."

"What was this nightmare about? Maybe it would help if you told me," his voice was always very comforting.

"I don't want to talk about it."

"You know, little tiger, when I was younger and couldn't sleep, I would try to think of good things and people like a pretty girl."

"What do you mean, Dad?"

"Why don't you think of the prettiest girl in your class and see if that helps?"

"I don't think it will help," I was also slightly embarrassed at this point that my dad was talking to me about girls, especially since I never told him I found any of my classmates attractive.

"Try it for your father."

"Okay, Dad, I will give it a try," I said with some hesitance.

I did manage to fall asleep after thinking of the cute girl in my class named Nicole. We had never really spoken, but she answered all the questions in class that the teacher would ask her so I figured she was cute and smart. I thought of her sitting in her desk raising her hand to get the teacher's attention and I drifted off to sleep.

The next morning, I awoke, barely ready to go to school. I knew the whole day I would be worried about my father and how and if he would get home all right. For the next few nights, I had recurring nightmares and was growing very anxious. I would pace in the early morning hours in my bedroom slightly tired from lack of sleep but full of racing thoughts of my dad crashing his Ford.

I hated school because of my mean teacher and had trouble concentrating on the tests because, in my mind, I could see my poor dad lying on the highway, bleeding all over, gasping for air. By Thursday, my teacher asked me if I was okay and I said I was because I did not feel comfortable speaking to her. When I went home, I watched some television but did not find it very soothing.

Nighttime quickly came and I went to bed before Dad got home from work. He was teaching an evening class that night. I was in bed, wishing I could just close my eyes and fall asleep but it wasn't happening. I could usually hear my dad pull into the driveway at this time. I was a little scared. I wondered if he had a crash and died. It was a possibility. A half-hour passed and so I went to see my mom in their bedroom. I told her of my fears even though I was scared of being yelled at by her.

"Mom, is Dad all right?"

"Yes, he is just running late. Go to bed."

"Mom, what if he gets into a car accident?"

"Your dad is an excellent driver. Please Steve, just let me get some rest," she put a novel in front of her face as she spoke to me.

"I love you, Mom," I said desperately.

"I love you too but I can't have you up at all hours of the night."

"What if Dad gets into an accident like Mr. Stein and dies?"

"He is not going to." She did not sound very convincing to me.

"How do you know, Mom?"

"I just do, Steve."

"Please Mom, tell me how you know he is not going to die."

"Are you all right, Steve?" Her voice was louder and sounded somewhat concerned for the first time, tonight.

Before I could press any further, I could hear my dad's car pull into the driveway so I scurried back to my room. I felt relieved temporarily of my fears and fell asleep moments later.

My dad, who was a stern but compassionate man, tried to talk to me the following morning. He told me that he loved me and that I would always be his little tiger. However, he also confided in me that he wasn't sure that he was best suited to help me. I didn't know exactly what he meant but thought he said something about a doctor before rushing out to the car. It was odd because my brothers didn't seem to have any problems during the night. Perhaps I was just overly sensitive.

For the next few weeks, things weren't getting any better. The majority of my days, whether in school or at home, were spent thinking about my nighttime problems. My parents didn't know how to solve the issue so they scheduled an appointment with a therapist for the following week.

The next Wednesday, instead of my usual walk from school back to my house, my mom picked me up from class and drove me to the appointment. We sat in the white dull-colored waiting room for about five minutes. I was very nervous since I had not really talked to anyone else about my fears. I had tried talking to my mom who I knew cared but she was awfully impatient.

A slender, attractive brunette came over and introduced herself as Ms. Grossman. She invited us into her office and explained that she was a social worker who helped children solve their problems. Hesitantly, I shared my feelings and she acknowledged that it was a legitimate fear. However, she cautioned, it should not dictate my life. According to her, a car accident could happen to anyone, but the odds were against it. Therefore, I should concentrate on the fact that my dad always came home. She reassured me that the odds were greatly in my dad's favor that he would return safely. It seemed logical but I had to ask her something.

"Ms. Grossman, what if the odds don't go in our favor. What if he does get into a car accident and he does die?"

She looked puzzled as if she didn't know what to say. I thought I saw her lips start to form a word but just stop as if she was completely stunned. She finally started to speak slowly and softly, "Steve, I know it's difficult for you but in life, we can't just be scared of things that have a small chance of occurring."

"I saw Noah today."

"Who is Noah?" she asked. At this point, I was growing more anxious as I noticed the therapist getting frustrated with my lack of understanding of her instructions.

My mom just sat next to me, looking impatient as well. She sighed after I mentioned Noah as if something bad was about to happen.

"Noah is the boy whose father died," I said.

"I'm so sorry for him but how is that affecting you when you see him?"

"I think of his father getting into a big crash and then I imagine my dad getting into a deadly crash as well."

"How often do you see him, Steve?"

"A couple of times a day when we pass in the hall."

"I'm sure Noah is going through a rough time but I'm here to make your days happier so let's concentrate on you."

I thought that was kind of selfish and was unsure what she wanted me to say. Also, worrisome for me, was that she seemed scared of what I might say.

"Right now, I'm having trouble concentrating on anything but my dad," I replied. I felt myself want to cry and hug my mother but she just buried her face in her hands as she rested them in her lap.

"I understand but I want to help."

"I'm not sure you can," I said in a strict tone that was unusual for me.

"Steve!" my mom shouted. "Don't talk that way to Ms. Grossman. She is a professional and wants to help you."

I felt my eyes start to twitch rapidly, as I was a bit shaken up.

"It's okay, Mrs. Goldberg, I think Steve has had a long day. It's fine if we end our session today and see each other next week."

"I'm sorry, Ms. Grossman," I nervously muttered, though I wasn't quite sure what I was sorry about.

"It's okay, Steve. I'm sorry I couldn't help you more but I think we will get through this with time. Would you like to come to see me next week?"

"Yes," I lied.

June 1980

The sessions with Ms. Grossman went on for a few months but they didn't accomplish much. After a brief period of time, my fears about my father dying in a car wreck started to go away. I started to relax a little bit both during the day and at night. My mother was able to see that I could go to bed and fall asleep without going into her room every night, further disturbing her. She stopped the sessions and my life went back to normal for a brief period of time. I was unable to realize at this young age that such fears would reappear, targeting my every weakness.

For the next few years, I would go to school, come home, and sometimes meet with friends that my mom would pick for me. However, I was never too happy about playing with friends and preferred to spend time at home. I was a loner even though my mom did not want to recognize this.

On weekends, sometimes my dad would toss the baseball around with me but he too preferred to stay inside. He was a loner as well and did not seem to have any friends of his own, unlike my mother. Rather than play baseball with me, we oftentimes stayed in and watched the Yankee games. I always enjoyed spending time with him even if we weren't actually doing much.

1983

I was now ten and maintained a group of friends that I would hang out with most of the time. Their names are unimportant since I didn't feel particularly close to any of them, nor did we stay in contact once high school began. When we did hang out, we would usually go to a candy store. It was at the candy store that my fears would escalate rapidly. I would usually find myself sitting on the floor of the aisle staring at the varieties of candy. At this point, an overwhelming, all-powerful force would occur to strike me. Though I had money and believed stealing was wrong, thoughts were creeping into my mind that I should take the candy. Then, I would get anxious and run out of the store before taking anything. I don't think any of my so-called friends realized I was going through a difficult situation. Again, I was completely unaware such rituals would darken every aspect of my life.

These ideas were ruminating in my head day after day, hour after hour, minute after minute. One night, I sought solace again from my mother which did not work out this time, either. I walked into her room where she was in bed reading, hoping she could say something that would reassure my troubled mind.

"Why are you still awake, Steve?" she quickly snapped at me.

"Mom, I think I'm a thief."

"You have never stolen anything, have you?"

"Of course not, Mom."

"Then where is this coming from?"

"When I go to the candy store with the guys, I feel an urge to put some of the Nestlé Crunch bars and Baby Ruths into my pockets and leave without paying."

"Why would you do that?" she seemed confused which resulted in me feeling stupid.

"I don't know. It's just a strong feeling I get."

"Steve, why don't you leave me alone and save this nonsense for your father?"

"It's not nonsense. It's how I feel!" I barked back.

"Don't raise your voice to me," she said coldly.

"Sorry."

"Do your tired mother a favor, Steve, and talk to your father when he gets home."

I desperately wanted to tell her all about the terrorizing thoughts and fears, hoping her words would comfort me. However, it seemed as if she was more concerned with getting a good night's rest than helping me. I loved her but couldn't really feel the same intimacy that I felt with my father. I decided before leaving that I would give her one last try.

"Mom, do you think other people my age feel this way about stealing?"

She replied with a notion which I didn't believe then or now: "All people feel that way, but the criminals are the ones who act out their desires and the good people fight off their impulses."

I nodded in agreement and returned to my room. I realized there was no help for me. My mom clearly didn't understand, and her senseless answers weren't helping. I lay in my bed for another ten minutes until I could hear my father's Ford pull up in the driveway. I had to talk to him to see what he thought.

When he entered the hallway, I yelled for him to come up and see me in my bedroom.

"How was your day, little tiger?" his face beaming with excitement.

"All right," I proceeded to tell him the events that were occurring at the candy store, and to my surprise, he understood.

"Steve, I think a lot of people like you feel that but they are scared to admit it. Remember, it's okay to think about these things and to talk with me about them."

"Dad, do you think Sam and Scott have the same feelings?"

"Everyone's different."

"But do you think when Sam takes Scott somewhere, they feel like stealing?"

"Well," he nervously uttered, "no, but they each have their own issues."

"What does that mean?"

"It means, Steve, that everyone has problems and your problems are different than your brothers', but it doesn't make you bad."

"If I stole, then I would be bad, right?"

"No, then you would have just made a mistake. But you would still be a good person. People are allowed to make mistakes and if you make one, just tell me and remember I love you."

"Dad, did you feel this way when you were my age?"

"You will understand more when you are older, Steve."

I did not know exactly what he meant but I felt reassured that he would always help me. Somehow, for the next several months, I was able to fight off my impulses at the candy store. Elementary school was a different and larger story.

1985

I would sit in my sixth-grade classroom wondering if Mrs. Cohen was going to approach me after dismissal. I had been a student at the same elementary school from kindergarten until now, where I was set to graduate. I had managed to hide my symptoms from both the students and my teachers. At least, I thought I had. However, maybe my teachers didn't want to get involved. I was fully aware that I had been making increasingly more body twitches and facial tics. Mrs. Cohen would often stare at me. I wanted her help, but she never offered any kind of assistance.

Yet, I was staring constantly at the ceiling from my third-row desk. I would start moving my nose in a strange way. I wanted to stop but felt an overriding urge to crinkle my nose. I also felt a similar impulse to scream but I knew if that happened, my mother would be disappointed. I would not let that happen, no matter how strong the urge. It did seem, however, that the students in the class were glued to Mrs. Cohen's lectures.

Children are often smarter than adults and I found that out one day during recess. Julie Silver approached me while I was calmly rocking back and forth alone at the swing set.

"Why do you do that thing with your nose, Steve?"

I was so alarmed that I couldn't say anything. I was scared that someone had found out my secret and my mind and body were racing for answers.

"Why, Steve?" she was persistent and was wearing an evil smile.

"I don't even know what you are talking about," I finally managed to say.

"Do it for me."

"Do what?"

"You know what I'm talking about. I see you all the time in class crunching your nose."

"I don't do anything like that," I was trying again to lie my way out of a difficult situation.

"Crinkle your nose for me like you do in Mrs. Cohen's class."

"Leave me alone."

"I just want to see you do it. It's funny."

I could hear our teacher yelling for us to come inside. I started to walk away from Julie when she said, "Steve, look at me."

I nervously glanced over and she was making the same movements with her nose that I would do all day in class. She was obviously able to stop when she wanted to, and was in complete control, unlike me. I started to feel myself get a little dizzy and physically shake. My eyes seemed to be twitching again. Julie must have become scared because she then ran toward the classroom.

I stood there shuddering and I still shudder now when I think about that incident. Julie and I never talked about anything like that again. My rituals would soon intrude on other aspects of my life.

One winter when I was about 11, schools were canceled due to snow. I was excited since it meant one less painful day. However, my father was home too and that morning, he was driven to get the driveway cleaned.

"Steve, I'm not going to ask you again; please help me shovel. Your brothers are away so I need your help."

"I don't want to," I just wanted to be left alone, as much as I loved my dad.

"I don't care. The cars need to be able to get out of the driveway."

I thought the whole thing was unfair. I was the only one being asked to do the shoveling because my older brother had slept over at a friend's house, and my younger brother was in bed with a virus. Things always went easier for them.

My dad was putting on a winter hat and gloves along with his oversized winter coat. I did not feel like shoveling. My older brother was with friends so why should I suffer by doing the work?

"I'll see you outside in a few minutes," he said as he slammed the door shut.

I could hear him checking from the outside that the door was locked, over and over again. My mom then walked into the kitchen where I was enjoying the waffles I had heated up.

"Please Steve, go help your father. He needs you."

"Why? I hate shoveling."

"Go help your father," she repeated.

I was in a horrific mood but got on the winter clothes that my mom had laid on my bed. I dressed quickly, hoping to get the work done already so I could go back to my waffles and watch television. When I came outside, my father was furiously shoveling the snow and was giving me directions where to shovel. It was as if our lives depended on it. After 20 minutes, I called it quits.

"Dad, I'm going in."

"What for?"

"Because the driveway is pretty clear."

"But there is ice."

"Dad, please don't ask me to crush the ice." It was difficult work and as usual, I was looking for an easy way out.

"Steve, get the ice pick out of the garage and help me break up the ice on the walkway so Mom doesn't fall."

He held the other ice pick in his hands and kept slamming away at it. He was strong—only 5'9" but a stout man who was physically able to do a lot of things.

"Dad, you are being silly. The ice will melt on its own."

"This will speed it up," he seemed really intent on getting everything done, and with my help.

"Dad, I'm not partaking in any of this nonsense."

"Just give me five minutes," he was pleading with me as if the world depended on breaking up the ice. It was odd to see my strong father appearing so weak.

"No," I was surprised at how firm my voice sounded, but I really just wanted a morning full of pancakes and television.

I walked back into the house, straight into the kitchen, and started to heat up the waffles that I had not finished eating. My mother followed behind me.

"Why are you not helping your father, Steve?"

"Shut up," I muttered but it was loud enough for her to hear me. I was in a lousy mood and was now scared of what was to come next.

"Don't tell me that, ever. There are murderers on death row who treat their mothers with more respect."

"Sorry," I said, knowing that I had messed up but also wishing that my mom was a more compassionate woman.

Ten minutes later, I could still hear my old man chipping away at the ice.

My mom opened the door and yelled out for him to come in.

"He's frantic," I said.

"Then help your father," she replied back quickly.

"I don't want to."

"Then you are spoiled. Now go help that man."

"No."

"You never do anything around here."

"I want to eat and rest."

"Your poor father is doing this alone and you're old enough to help."

I knew she was right. I was a spoiled, angry child and I was sick and tired of having to do things I hated. I loved my father but hated living.

As my mom walked out of the house to bring my father back inside, she said, "You are no use to us right now, and yet you have so much potential. It's very sad." If her intent was to make me feel any worse than I did a few minutes earlier, she had indeed succeeded.

About 15 minutes later, after my mom had pleaded with my father to come in and rest, he finally did so.

I was in the kitchen eating my waffles. I glanced at my dad who had just put away his jacket in the family closet and was now sitting, slightly slouched in a chair in the living room. He didn't look too content but I didn't think much of it as I walked away. A few seconds later, I had a bad feeling because all I could sense was silence.

"Dad."

There was no answer and my mom was now lying upstairs in bed reading the paper.

"Dad?" my anxiety grew and I felt a horrible pit in my stomach.

Again, no answer. I turned to walk toward his chair and saw that he was slouched even more in the seat he occupied and his eyes were shut. I knew he was dead as I approached him and put my cold hands on his arms trying to see if there was any feeling in his body. I felt nothing.

"Mom!" I screamed.

"What is it now?"

"Dad's not moving. I think he is dead," I didn't think I sounded that alarming but rather calm. Either way, my mother practically flew down the stairs to assist her husband.

"Bob, Bob!" she was shouting and I was becoming more scared. I was certain that he was dead.

She started to pull him from his chair by his arms but I then turned away. I couldn't take any more of this level of living. There was just too much misery and nervousness for me to face and now I would have to face the rest of my life without my best friend. I, therefore, turned my face away from what was going on and walked downstairs to the television room.

"Bob!" she shouted his name so loudly that I figured our neighbors might be able to hear. My dad, who was desperate for my assistance with the ice a half-hour ago, was now in the hands of his desperate wife.

Finally, I heard something encouraging.

"Sorry honey!" I heard him say slowly to my mother. I then walked back up the stairs, feeling slightly better but knowing that in the midst of a crisis, I was nowhere to be found.

"What happened?" she said as I watched from the hallway, about 15 feet away.

"I don't know. I just feel out of breath. I just need to rest."

My dad pulled himself up while remaining sitting, but no longer slouched in his favorite chair. My mom walked briskly toward the kitchen to grab my dad some coffee.

"See what you did," my mom pointed out, as I could feel her disgust staring at me.

"I'm sorry," I wasn't sure what else I could do at this moment. My self-worth was low when I woke this morning, and now I felt even worse.

"Go tell that to him."

I walked over to my father who looked worn out but was breathing fine.

It was as if my father had not even realized how close to death he had come. I remembered back to a time when I was a child at a diner with my family. There was a young, skinny boy at the table next to us, and he began choking on his steak. At the time, while everyone else in the restaurant was paralyzed with fear, my dad calmly got out of his seat. He went toward the child and proceeded to give him the

Heimlich maneuver until the piece of steak was ejected from his mouth. The boy's family was so relieved and was eager to congratulate my father for saving their son's life. My dad wanted nothing to do with the handshakes or hugs. He simply got out of the family's way and returned to our table, eager to finish his chocolate ice cream and head home. It was like a chore to him rather than a miraculous feat. It was just something he did and wanted to carry on with his day as if nothing of importance happened. That was the way my dad had always been. He wanted no special attention and he put on no airs about himself, either. This is how he seemed at that moment. He didn't desire any special attention for doing all the shoveling while I stayed inside. He just wanted to go on as if it was any other ordinary day.

"I'm sorry, Dad," I wanted to hug him but did not think he would want my embrace.

"It's okay, son."

"Are you all right?"

"I think so."

"I..." I couldn't finish the sentence.

"What?"

I wanted to tell him I loved him but just could not do it. I could tell my mom I loved her, even when she was furious with me. But telling my father—now that was completely different.

"Just that I'm sorry, Dad."

"It's okay, Steve. I love you," he smiled and looked so sweet, I wanted to try to hug him again.

"I will shovel next time."

"I know you will, little tiger," he seemed so proud of being my father, and yet I felt like I had failed again.

I couldn't say the words and I was as much ashamed at myself for that as for not helping my dad with the ice. As usual, when I wanted to express something, whether it would be soliciting help from one of my teachers or telling my dad my true feelings, I hid in shame from those closest to me.

The next morning, there was a loud knock on my bedroom door. I came out of the room and saw my older brother looking straight at me. He looked very disappointed. I was very intimidated by him, even though he was just a few inches taller than me. I was always somewhat fearful of him because he didn't say much to me.

"I want to speak to you, Steve. Be in my room in the next minute."

I was startled. I had just woken up and now Sam wanted to have a confrontation. It was obvious that he had heard about the shoveling incident. I wanted to tell him to fuck off but instead just remained silent.

My heart was beating fast. I wanted to get this conversation over with so I ran into his room which was adjacent to mine.

"Sit down," he said.

"Thank you," I managed to say as my heart was pounding out of my chest.

I sat down on the sofa and he remained standing. He started talking but I was struggling to hear him.

I heard something about Dad, and so I tried to tune in.

"Can you repeat what you just said, Sam?"

"I said that if you want to put Mom and Dad's health at risk, I will hurt you."

The conversation had made an immediate downward spiral as my brother wanted to pummel me.

"Don't touch me, Sam. I don't even know what you have against me." I realized after I said this that he had not moved an inch closer to me. Yet, I immediately feared violence. Sam had only struck me on a few occasions. However, we had rarely been in the same room together during the last few years. He would pass by me in school and not even acknowledge me. Yet, it did hurt my feelings. I always wondered why he was so cold to me.

But my dad told me when I asked why he didn't like me, that Sam was sorting things out.

That did not make it any easier and I thought things would have changed by now. The last time Sam and I spent any time together, things did not go so well. That was the previous winter and probably the reason why I feared him.

Sam asked me to play with some of his friends in a pickup football game at a field near our old elementary school. It was only because my mother had asked him to do her a favor, I later found out.

It was just supposed to be a fun game of touch football, but I was hesitant to play as I was not very athletic.

During the game, I was pretty much left alone until a friend of Sam's tackled me as a pass was surprisingly thrown my way. He hit me in the chest and I felt my knees buckle. I was unable to hold onto the football. His friend started to laugh at me and called me a "faggot," as I fell to the ground.

That was the worst thing you could be called and I started to twitch like a little kid in my elementary classroom.

My head was twitching back and forth, from side to side, and others noticed.

"Hey Sam, your brother is a retard. Just look at the way he moves like one. No wonder you never bring him around," he said with a big grin. He was then laughing hysterically as if he was watching a comedy routine. But I was not a comic, just a teenager trying to make it through another tough day with slightly older boys.

I wanted desperately for Sam to come to my rescue but I was quickly disappointed. He ran over to me, and the sense of hate and embarrassment that was in his eyes was obvious. "Maybe Sam is a retard," the boy said to my brother. Sam pushed the boy away from me so it was just us looking at each other.

He slapped my face quickly. I was shocked but even more so by what he said immediately after. "You are a freak, Steve."

"I'm sorry, Sam," I cried as I feared more punches would come. I was trapped and didn't know what to do next. I was too scared to leave, especially since I walked to the field with my older and more respected brother. I just stood there, staring at my brother, bracing for another slap. I saw him clench his fist tightly. He was too smart to leave a mark on my face which would require an explanation to our parents. Instead, he laid one into my stomach so hard that I had the wind knocked out of me and fell to the floor. I was not only physically hurt but in agony over his betrayal.

"I'm no retard and definitely not a faggot. Now, get out of here," he said with hate still in his eyes. I left the schoolyard but never said anything to my parents for two reasons. One, that I didn't think they would believe me, and second, that I didn't want to push my luck with Sam.

"I will hurt you. Do you hear me, Steve?" Sam said as I tried to focus. I was immediately drawn back to the present where I was engaged in a dangerous conversation with my brother.

"I understand," I nervously uttered. "But why, why Sam do you want to hurt me?"

"Listen, Steve, I'm not going to be drawn into some long conversation regarding this. It's difficult enough to be in the same school as you."

I was only slightly surprised. I always figured he didn't like me but didn't think he gave the matter much thought.

"You don't even talk to me when you see me," I said with some anger that even startled me.

"I've learned through the years, Steve, to stay away from you."

"I just want to know why," my voice was starting to crack as if tears were coming on, but I persisted. "Why?" I said louder.

"Because you are sick."

I was desperate to know how he knew this. Some of my actions in school were strange to others but I never really thought Sam had noticed anything. Perhaps, he had seen me twitching all this time when I was in school. Either way, it didn't really matter. He didn't want to have much to do with me, and now I completely understood.

I wanted to cry but this was not the time, so I held it together. I needed to be strong, even if it killed me.

"What does this have to do with Mom and Dad?"

"It has everything to do with them," he said in a stern but low voice. I was amazed at his ability to say such horrible things without raising his voice. I wondered whether my parents were downstairs eating breakfast and whether they realized we were speaking.

"It was an accident what happened to Dad. I didn't mean for anything bad to happen. Besides, Mom shouldn't have said anything to you."

"Settle down, Steve. Just listen and be quiet."

"What do you want, Sam?"

"I'll make it simple. Stay away from me and Scott."

"So why are you speaking with me?" I asked.

"To let you know that I am aware of everything that occurred yesterday. And that if you put any of us in harm's way again, I will destroy you."

"Thanks for your honesty," I said in a sarcastic tone that even surprised me. But I realized the worst was over. I then got off the sofa and walked quickly back to my bedroom where I lay in bed. I was desperate for some peace from my wandering mind that was more focused on the significance of the past than the present situation.

My memory was pushed back again to an earlier time with Sam and a boy named Joseph Fried when we were both in elementary school. My brother had been being picked on by this classmate and he cried to my father one night about how he was being bullied by Joseph. My father told him that he had to face his fears and fight Joseph. The following morning, my brother walked to school early and by the time I got there, I was able to see my brother kicking the bully in the stomach.

Joseph was crying on the ground, begging for Sam to stop. My brother looked completely in control at the time and nobody messed with him again. I admired him at the time.

As I lay back in bed, facing both the present time and the ceiling, I wanted to cry. I desperately used all my will to prevent tears from coming down my face.

I also thought about telling my parents what had just occurred. They both wouldn't believe me and I would probably be the one who looked out of control. Sam, though, would most likely remain steady and composed, just like he did when he stood over a wounded Joseph Fried years earlier.

He was always cool and he wanted to have nothing to do with me. He thought of me as an infectious disease that could spread throughout the family, particularly to my little brother Scott.

I wasn't sure what bothered him most about me. I realized it would be pointless to try to get Sam to open up more about his problems with me. He wanted to tell me just the necessary info to keep me away from him. As much as I was upset with the way he spoke to me, I still maintained an odd admiration for him. He didn't like me but I wanted to be just like him. He was cool, calm, and collected. My mind kept flashing back to earlier times when I was in elementary school and Scott was a toddler.

The memories that appeared before me were of us all as a family eating supper with my parents.

However, there was never much interaction between myself and my two brothers. I wanted a relationship with them but it did not look now as if that would ever happen.

This saddened me greatly as I continued to stare at the ceiling in my bedroom while still lying down.

I began to feel nauseous as the idea that I would never have a meaningful relationship with either brother was a harsh rejection for me, and possibly the strongest one I ever suffered. My stomach was now feeling ill as I could hear it rumbling around, wanting to vomit. I became scared and ran for the bathroom where I vomited my last night's supper into the toilet.

A moment later, I began to clean both the toilet and myself up when I heard my mom yelling from downstairs.

"Steve, are you okay?"

I exited the bathroom and walked downstairs, wanting to confront her.

"Were you throwing up?" she asked with surprising compassion.

"Yes, but where is Dad?"

"He went with Sam and Scott to the mall."

"I will talk to Dad later."

"Steve, you can talk to me about why you are sick," she said with a tone that was very different than the way she used with me yesterday.

"Mom, why did you tell Sam about yesterday?" I asked with some fear of what was to come. I did not want to have a second confrontation this early in the morning, but I was at a crossroads over where I stood in this family. I knew my dad loved me but didn't understand much else.

"Steve, there's not really much to tell."

"How do you mean?" I said, very confused.

"I just told him the truth when he came home yesterday and asked how the day went."

"Well, this morning he told me to stay away from him and Scott."

"So what?" she said, rather stoically.

"How can you say it like that, Mom?"

"I'm just calling it like it is. You never really bonded with either of them," she approached me and put her hand on my back. I wasn't sure if she wanted me to hug her or not, but I resisted.

I was stunned to hear my mom say such things with a mild voice. She wasn't acting as if there was a major problem in the house, but just a minor issue.

I thought about telling her more since she was warmer to me than she had been in some time.

"Steve, you have two parents that care about you even when you are not easy, which is often. So what is the difference if your older brother is disappointed in you?"

"He has no right to be," I said sternly.

"Sam doesn't see it that way."

"It's not his business."

I wanted to tell her that Sam threatened me with violence and that he saw me as some kind of monster.

I knew that would be taking things too far. It would tear the family apart and I would be in further isolation. She had removed her hand from my back and now stood right by me. I wanted to embrace her but that would be too big of a step. I probably would also cry if I told her the cold truth about Sam.

I wondered if my relationships with Sam and Scott could ever be fixed.

"It's not his business," I repeated hoping for an explanation.

"You can't fix this, Steve."

"Do you think Sam will ever change his mind about me, Mom?"

"I don't know and it doesn't matter. I just need you, Steve, to try to listen to your father and me."

"I could do that, Mom," I wanted desperately to satisfy her since I couldn't please my older brother.

"Can you? Because you are a very stubborn child."

"I don't try to be."

"I have to realize that you are indeed not trying to be stubborn," she said, and then paused for a moment. "Do you love me, Steve?" It was a question usually reserved just for holidays.

"Yes," I said immediately.

At least, I thought I did because that is what sons told their mothers in normal families. This was not a normal family. In normal families, older brothers did not threaten their younger brothers with violence because they viewed them as off or embarrassing.

"Thank you, Steve. I want you to know that sometimes I can't help but lose patience with you but I am trying to work on it. Don't give up on me, Son."

I was genuinely touched by her openness, "I won't, Mom."

Hebrew School – 1984

My mother would practically tie me to the back of the car to get me to go to Temple. I hated Hebrew School and all the teachers. I was hardly able to read the language and questioned the practicality of comprehending a dead language. What was the point of being forced to learn a language if we were not taught what it meant? However, being raised in a Jewish home, both my parents wanted me to excel in this area. I did not know if they knew how mean the staff was to me and that I was always disappointing them.

I also couldn't stand the arrogant Rabbi Feldman who always drove to his fancy home in a BMW. One Sunday morning, I was terrorized by Rabbi Feldman. He came into the classroom to give a lecture on why Judaism was prospering while Christianity was built on mistaken beliefs. Feldman elaborated that since Jesus was not the savior, Christianity was not only a flawed religion but a phony one as well. I thought it was peculiar that Feldman was so strident against other religions. He preached about us being receptive to new ideas but his mind was so closed about other religions. Surely at Christian schools, they didn't talk badly about Jews, I figured. I just wanted to have my Bar-Mitzvah and be free of this terrible school.

I was a few years away from my goal and was still forced to endure his wrath. That morning, during his presentation, I was bored with his lecture so my mind began to wander. I started to think about going home and watching the Yankee game with my father. I didn't think Feldman would catch on so I started flipping through my baseball cards. Feldman must have noticed because I could hear his footsteps getting closer to my desk. I looked away from the cards and saw that he was very angry as his face had reddened. Suddenly, as our eyes met, I heard him scream, "Why are you playing with baseball cards when you are at my synagogue?" He took the cards and threw them on the floor. I was shocked and scared at both loudness of his voice and the actions that followed. The only person I knew who could scream as loudly was my mother. I felt a stirring in my stomach as if I was going to vomit.

"Now, pick them up," he demanded.

I paused for a few seconds as I was fearful of him but was embarrassed enough to make a public stand.

"You threw them so you pick them up," I said in a low voice.

"What did you say?" he asked.

I didn't have the guts to repeat my words and so I cowered in defeat and shrugged my shoulders.

Rabbi Feldman appeared shocked and ordered me to go to his office.

There, he lowered his voice and said, "Your behavior today is not worthy of this school so I am going to call your father."

As I sat in a cheap fold-up chair, I was just hoping that my dad would answer the call rather than my mother. He was always better at dealing with my problems. The rabbi went into an adjacent room and dialed my house number. I couldn't hear the conversation but knew it wouldn't go over well with either of my parents.

An hour later, my father was forced to pick me up from the office.

My dad looked pale when he arrived and just stared at me. The rabbi said something to him but he was so disappointed, he must have been speechless. A few moments later, he was able to speak.

"I am so sorry, Rabbi. I just want my son to learn about Judaism and become more actively involved in his religion but he seems interested in only his secular hobbies. I will talk to him," explained my loving dad. The rabbi nodded in agreement, shook my father's hand, and told him to have a safe ride home.

When I arrived home, I told my father that the Rabbi called Christianity a "phony" religion. My dad explained to me that Rabbi Feldman is very passionate about Judaism but he should not have used those words.

"They're not bad people."

"Who?" I asked.

"Christians; they just have a different belief system." It seemed to me that my father had a more gentle opinion of other religions than the strict Feldman.

"So you like Christians?" I asked curiously.

"Of course, Stevie, I like all people who are good to one another."

"So could I ask you something else?" I asked timidly.

"Go ahead."

"Do you believe in Jesus?" I was at first surprised to hear that question come out of my mouth but it was something I had been meaning to ask my father since I started Hebrew School.

"He existed," he said rather unemotionally.

"I know, but do you worship him?"

"It doesn't matter."

"It does to me," I said because everyone in Hebrew School taught me that we rejected him as our lord.

Of course, it mattered because that is what made us different than other religions. Also, my dad was always fighting for Jewish causes. How could he not see that this was an important matter?

"Dad, what do you mean?"

"Let me watch the game," he said as he lay back in his chair trying to watch his favorite sport.

"Dad, please tell me if you worship Jesus."

"Son, I'm not going to discuss this further. Please go to your room and think about how you behaved today."

"But—" I muttered but he shut me up quickly.

"Enough," he said. His voice seemed irritated.

"Why won't you talk to me?" I replied.

"Why does it matter so much, Steve?" he seemed clueless as to why it would matter to me and I felt like giving him a piece of my mind just as I did with Feldman earlier.

"Dad, I hate the synagogue and yet you make me go there and you don't understand why it matters to me if you believe in Jesus."

"Stevie," he said softly, "your job is to behave in that school and not embarrass the Goldberg reputation that your dear mother and I have tried to build in this community. Now there is no further conversation needed at this time."

I thought about responding to his demand but I knew it would only lead to trouble. I did not, for the life of me, understand why my dad was so hesitant to tell me his beliefs.

Years later, my dad grew tired of the growing costs of belonging to Feldman's congregation and switched me to a different Hebrew School where I had a Bar Mitzvah. When I was leaving the temple with my dad one day after he had a disagreement with the Rabbi and informed him of our intent to leave, Feldman told me that he would miss me.

"As your first spiritual leader, I will always be there for you throughout your life," he said to me as we were all outside the temple as my dad was trying to get me to go quickly to the car and leave for the last time.

"Now is not the time to talk to my son," my dad pointed out.

"I just want him to know that there is always a place for him here."

"He understands that perfectly," said my father whose anger baffled me as it seemed at the time that Rabbi Feldman actually did like me.

I always remembered that seemingly sympathetic conversation because years later while I was struggling with my illness, I called Feldman for guidance. Sadly, he never returned my call. I pleaded with his receptionist to have him contact me but he never did.

The High School Years

I was always close to missing the bus that took me to my dreaded high school which I hated. I despised the students who bullied me and the teachers that tolerated it. Nobody cared about anyone. Teachers would watch students fall to pieces and sit by silently. It was torture. Likewise, so were my morning rituals. I would shower for approximately 40 minutes, eat, and then do some more washing. It was particularly my hands, though I did rewash other parts of my body. I believed that my hands were contaminated with HIV. I did not want it on my conscience if I infected someone which led to their death. The worst thing in the world was to be a murderer.

It was a tough period for our country as the U.S. was struggling with the AIDS epidemic. The media and the teachers all said that we could only get AIDS if we were gay, or shared needles while taking drugs. I was not gay nor would I ever think of doing drugs, but I was still afraid. Somehow, I believed that if I touched an object that was previously touched by an infected person, I could pass on that infection to others. Even if it was a mere handshake, if my hands were contaminated, I would be spreading AIDS and killing people. I felt horrible about the idea of being a killer and would go to no ends to try to protect people. This is why I was always washing my hands. Ironically, I washed them so much that I would walk around the school with dry, chapped hands that were sometimes so red that they bled. It didn't matter though since I had no friends and no one really wanted to talk with me.

I had picked up new rituals during high school that replaced the old problems from when I was a child in elementary school. I wasn't twitching or shaking in my seat but when I met my new English teacher in junior year, some of the problems resurfaced. Mrs. Williams was a black woman. I didn't have anything against her, although I lived in an all-white town. At least, I didn't think I had any feelings of ill-will. However, the "n" word was on my lips and I had frequent compulsions to yell out the word during class. I don't think I ever actually said that harmful word, but it was a struggle to keep my lips shut.

My dad once told me when I was a kid that the word was never to be spoken as it was a sign of prejudice and racism. While I was in her class, I took all of my father's words to heart and was scared that I was a racist or a bigot.

I thought I was a fair-minded individual but the fact that I was compelled to say that ugly word caused me much worry. *Who was I?* I asked myself as I feared I was no better than the white supremacist skinheads my dad railed against during political conversations, Sunday night at the dinner table.

Mrs. Williams was kind and I thought about telling her about the problem one afternoon as she stopped me as I was leaving her room.

"Is everything all right, Steve?" she asked compassionately.

"Why do you ask?"

I was torn because I wanted to leave the classroom without getting in trouble for using the n-word but I also had a deep desire to unload my troubles. Mrs. Williams was one of the kinder teachers in the school. If ever there was an opportunity to connect with a teacher, now was the time.

"Steve, you looked troubled in class today. Is there anything you want to tell me?" I noticed that she wore her hair down and looked pretty even if she was just wearing jeans. I felt somewhat guilty for finding her attractive as I was told by my peers back in Hebrew School that I should only be interested in Jewish girls. I knew though that as pretty as Mrs. Williams was and being only in her late 20s, she had a family and was just concerned for my well-being.

"Everything is fine, Mrs. Williams. Thank you," I felt the need to leave her classroom right away.

I was starting to walk out of the empty classroom again when she persisted.

"Steve, don't shut me out," I was taken aback by how candid she was. Most teachers in the school were just biding time, trying to get through the day. They didn't really care about making a difference.

"I'm not. I just have to go," I lied.

"Steve, it's the last period of the day and I'm going to insist that you speak with me for a few minutes."

"I'm doing okay in the class, aren't I?"

"That is not it," she said.

"What do you want?" I had become more direct in my conversations with authority over the years. I was still timid but had the where with all to make sure I wasn't trapped in a losing battle.

"I want to know why you look so upset during class and seem to be stopping yourself from saying something." I began to worry that she had heard me use the expletive and that I had been unable to control my mouth and tongue. My greatest fear was losing control. I was scared to lose control of every facet of my life. I was feeling compelled to say the bad word again but I felt overwhelmed by her speech.

"Talk to me, Steve."

"There is nothing to talk about," I felt on the one hand that she was trying to expose me and on the other hand that I can really speak to this compassionate woman.

"You don't want to talk about the fact that you are a junior and it seems like you have no friends in this school." Again, I was shocked at how direct she was, especially about topics that others never addressed.

"Why do you care? You are my teacher. I'm doing the classwork adequately." My voice was stern.

I was feeling nauseous again since I hated confrontation but since she was an adult, I knew I would have a tough time getting out of this confrontation. I despised confrontations just as I did when my older brother years ago told me I was sick.

"I care, Steve, because I'm not only a teacher but a human being as well. What do you think of the faculty here? Do you think we all just go along to get along? That we are just here to teach our classes and everyone should hide behind their job descriptions?"

"That seems to me, Mrs. Williams, pretty par for the course."

"I'm sorry you feel that way but the buck stops with me today." I felt comforted by her no holds barred, empathetic approach with me. It was different but she was beautiful and compassionate.

"What do you want me to say, Mrs. Williams?"

"I want you to answer some of my questions."

Again, I was torn. I didn't want to say too much because I was afraid she might tell some of the administrators about me, but on the other hand, she seemed so concerned and genuine that I felt like possibly talking to her.

"I will try to answer some of your questions," I politely replied as I was feeling more at ease with her,

"It's December, Steve, so I should have asked you this earlier in the school year and for that, I apologize, but why are your hands all cut up and red, as if they have been bleeding?"

She cut right to the chase and I was somewhat attracted to her perceptiveness. We had never had a conversation like this before though my paranoia sometimes believed she was looking at me during her lectures.

"It's winter and it's cold outside so my skin gets irritated." That was the first and only thing I could think of saying.

"You must have really sensitive skin because no one else in the class suffers like that from the weather."

"That is all I can tell you, Mrs. Williams."

"So it's going to be that way, huh Steve?"

"I don't know what you are talking about," I lied again. I often played hard and fast with the truth as avoiding it was often in my best interest,

"Yes, you do, but you don't want to be candid with me."

I was feeling pains in my stomach now and as much as I liked Mrs. Williams, I had to get out of this confrontation. What at one moment seemed like empathy, now felt like a situation that could only lead to me saying too much.

"Can I go now?" I asked.

"I'm not finished." I could tell that she was getting agitated but she persisted with me.

"One more question, Steve, and then you can go home and hide."

I resented her choice of words as well as her condescending tone. I felt myself enraged like a prizefighter in the ring who had just been hit for the first time.

"Mrs. Williams, you are not my mom and I don't have to take this. I'm not hiding from anyone. It's the faculty and everyone in this school who hides from everything including me. Pardon my language, but nobody gives a fuck about me."

"So the truth finally reveals itself, Steve. You hate this school," she remained calm even in the face of my anger.

"You are damn right and I can't wait until I go off to college."

"So you think everything is going to change for you once you leave this area? I hate to tell you this, Steve, but the world doesn't work like that, for you or anyone."

"Well, I'm sure as hell going to try."

"I'm sorry I have made you upset, Steve, but at least I see now that there is some passion in your belly. If only you would tell me more, I could help. I know the faculty can seem stern but not all of us are like that. Believe me, I know what it's like to be different here."

I was feeling less intense and my little burst of rage had subsided. I was shocked that Mrs. Williams, my English teacher, was allowing me into her private life. "I'm sorry I cursed. Please don't turn me in," I begged.

"I'm glad you opened up a bit. I just wish you would trust me a little more. And I don't turn friends in."

I wondered if she actually saw me as a friend for the first time or whether she was just trying to manipulate me like Rabbi Feldman on my last day at the Temple. However, after that quick thought, I felt led to believe she was sincere.

"What else do you want to know?" I asked, but this time hoping she might get me to speak more.

"Well, Steve, it seems like you are struggling to say something in class. It seems like you have an urge to say something but you are holding back. What do you want to say?"

"Nothing."

"Steve, we are past that. What is it that you want to say that you are scared of saying?"

I couldn't believe this teacher, this magnificent woman, was so able to connect with me. I felt almost completely at ease with her. She wanted to help me. After all these years of struggling in school with bad thoughts, evil tics, and disgusting words, I was at a crossroads. I could tell her everything and she might help me or have some answers that I was looking for. However, on the other hand, I was fully aware that speaking to her just a little bit would lead me to tell her everything in my life—not just school, but all my problems. She wanted to help but I still was reluctant to open the pandora's box. As much as I felt at ease with her, my fear persisted like a thorn in my side telling me she would inform the administrators, school psychologists, and others which would lead to my parents being brought into the school for a meeting. I didn't think my mom could handle this since she wanted to fit in with everyone in this affluent town. And again, as much as I had little social contact with my peers and teachers, I wanted desperately not to stand out.

"Mrs. Williams, I appreciate everything you are trying to do but I can't go any further."

"Can't or won't, Steve?"

"It's the same thing to me, unfortunately."

"That is unfortunate, Steve. I hope you find someone soon who you can open up to."

"Oh, I have, when I'm ready, Mrs. Williams." She smiled and it warmed my heart to see that she enjoyed getting through to me.

"Then we will speak again, Steve?"

"Well, I will see you in class every day."

"You know what I mean."

"I do but I can't promise that we will speak like this again. Only, that when I'm ready, I know you are here for me."

I had one last temptation to tell this beautiful woman everything that was going on with me from my obsession with the AIDS crises to my constant battle against germs. I figured, though, that I could always talk to her again when I was ready. However, once again, I was scared to test the waters and expand my horizons. Instead, I stayed shut off from my peers, teachers, and even my true self.

That conversation with this magnanimous teacher was the last candid conversation I had with her. We would continue to smile at each other in class and I felt a strong connection with her spiritually, but I never got around to talking to her again that year. I always thought I would have more time, or that possibly I could speak to her the following year before graduation. However, I learned right after my junior year that she was denied tenure and was seeking employment closer to her home. I never knew for sure the real reason why she was denied tenure but I could imagine the cause. I also could still hear her telling me, "I know what it's like to be different here."

Summer Day Camp

As much as I hated school, I loved summer camp. I went there from the time I was six to when the camp closed down the summer before I was to go away to college. Maybe it was because I had been there so long or because it was located in North Jersey, but no one there would have suspected that I was suffering from social problems at school. They didn't know me at school nor would they take the time to understand me, or at least that is what I concluded. They liked me here, and each summer, I became increasingly more popular. My personality and sense of humor were able to develop each summer. I bet most of my camp friends assumed I was popular at school. It struck me as odd that someone could be two different people so early on in life.

Even the girls found me cute. I remember the first time a young girl had a crush on me. We were both 12 years old and this cute girl named Lisa was on a scavenger hunt with her counselors to find the cutest boy in the camp.

She approached me in late August and yelled out, "Steve, you are the cutest boy in this camp."

"Who are you?" I replied, not knowing her name, but liking what I saw.

"Lisa, you stud," she was grinning and had a great smile.

"What is it you want, Lisa?" I was confident that she did like me.

"You."

"Why?"

"You are the cutest boy I know and I want you to be my boyfriend."

"That's a lot to ask," I was only 12 but I was bold at camp. If a similar situation had occurred at my school, I would probably have run away.

"How do you know me?" I asked.

"I've been watching you play softball and you have cute legs. I asked my counselor to find out your name and that is all there is to it."

I was extremely flattered because I knew I wasn't a great athlete and had never looked at any part of my body as being attractive or fit. No girls at school ever said that I was cute and my parents or relatives never mentioned my looks at all. I thought of myself as average height and slightly chubby though it was hard for me to really know how I looked to others. I often stared at myself in the mirror but was never sure if the truth was being accurately reflected back to me.

"It's the last week of camp. What has taken you so long to approach me?" I asked.

"I could ask the same thing of you but I never see you talking with girls. Anyways, I'm on a scavenger hunt with my counselor who asked me to find the cutest boy in camp."

"And you think that is me?"

"I know it is."

I knew that she was only 12 but that confidence of hers really made me find her sexy. She was more daring than anyone I had encountered. I had lots of male friends at the camp but she was the first girl that told me I was cute. I was at a loss over what to say so I just paused and she continued in her sassy way.

"Well, do you think I'm cute?" she asked.

I still didn't know what to say so I just stared at her beautiful face and said nothing. I didn't know where this was going to lead, but I was taken by her attractiveness and willing to let her make the first and every move.

"Well, if you don't think I'm cute, Steve, I will just leave you here to hang out with your counselors."

"I didn't say that," I definitely did not want her to leave.

"What are you saying?"

"I'm not sure."

I was certainly a bit nervous but none of my ticks were flaring up. Perhaps I was so caught up in the moment that I didn't have a chance to think about anything else but Lisa.

"Do you want me to leave, Steve?"

"No."

"So tell me what you think of me."

"I think you are very cute," I almost laughed as I had never had such an intimate conversation with a girl at the time. She was awfully flirtatious and I liked it very much.

"Good, because I was afraid for a second you didn't like me."

"No, I do," I stated quickly.

"Good, I'm glad that is established. Now, do you want to go take a hike with me into the woods for a little while?"

My heart was beating fast as I didn't know what to say. I was feeling slightly brave, though. Maybe because it was becoming obvious that someone really did like me. She was so cute, complete with dimples and short hair which made her look unique.

"Yes, I would like that."

Both her and my counselors agreed that we could go into the woods together, as they were only 16 and didn't care much for rules. I was very nervous, but the excitement of entering those woods alone with her was something I couldn't pass up. The woods were well known for the stories of different Native-American tribes living there, though nobody had ever witnessed one. There were also stories of killings that led to the mystique of the woods. However, I never previously entered them before.

Lisa and I walked up the trail and found an old red bench to sit on.

"You're very beautiful," I said. I had said that only because I thought I was supposed to and had seen it said on different television shows. However, it was far from a lie.

She leaned toward me and kissed my lips gently. We struggled for a few seconds until our mouths joined and it felt like heaven. I loved kissing her but doubted I was the first boy she had been with.

"You're so cute, Steve. Do you want to go further?" She too was bold, a little too bold so I pulled back from her.

Terrified, I said, "No, I'm not ready."

We kissed a few more times, but I could never go beyond kissing, knowing that God and my mother would disapprove if I moved anywhere beyond first base. My mom had told me when I was about seven that there was good touching and bad touching. She added that nobody except family was supposed to touch me and I couldn't even let friends touch me in private areas. I was unsure at the time why she told me this. I think she was afraid someone may have been touching me in school but neither of us took the conversation further. She ended the conversation one Saturday morning by saying, "If anyone does anything like that, Steve, tell me or your father right away. You don't want to upset me or God."

Anyway, Lisa soon dumped me, but I couldn't stop thinking about her every night. I was obsessed with her. However, camp ended and I was forced to think often of her into early October while sitting bored in class, where again my tics would flare up.

Regrettably, Lisa Gold never returned to camp the following summer. I never saw her again, though there were rumors years later that she was very promiscuous at her high school in Bergen County, New Jersey. I had met a few young girls the following summers and was becoming more confident with the opposite sex at camp.

At the age of 16, I met Sally who was a pretty redhead. She constantly flirted with me, though she told me she had a boyfriend at home. He apparently worked at a clothing store during the day and she saw him frequently. At least, that is what she told me. I didn't know if it was the truth or just something to make me jealous. Regardless, one Friday in mid-July, she asked if I would like to go into the woods. At the age of 16, I had realized the true purpose of the woods and had gone there with a few other females since Lisa. I still did not let it go beyond kissing.

It didn't take long before Sally and I were sucking face.

"So, you have a boyfriend?" I asked as I pulled away for a second.

"He is not here so let's continue with what we are doing and not talk about him."

"Are you in love with him?"

"What does it matter?"

"I just want to know," I was desperate to know more since I could feel myself having more significant feelings for her. I couldn't lose her. The smell of her hair, her perfume, it was all so intoxicating to me.

"I just want to be with you right now, is that all right?" she said, with a forcible tone.

I submitted and said yes, and we continued to make out for a few minutes. Then, all of a sudden, she led my hands to her chest and let me caress her. I was excited but very scared that I had done something wrong. At this point in my life, I had heard enough stories about other kids my age having sex that I didn't think the words of caution said by my mother years earlier applied anymore.

"Are you okay?" I asked her.

"Yes."

"Are you sure?"

I could feel the need to wash my hands come upon me. I had never touched anyone in that way and felt the need to wash my hands. I was becoming less like the popular boy at camp and more like the shy, awkward person that everyone saw at school.

We started kissing again while I caressed her but I paused and asked again, "Are you okay?"

"What is your problem?" she angrily replied.

I didn't know what to say or do but I could feel my nose twitching. I don't know if she noticed but she quickly responded, "I don't think you are ready for this, Steve. You are a nice boy but you are too immature for me. My boyfriend is not like this."

I felt seriously wounded at this point. I then turned away from her and ran out of the woods to the closest bathroom I could find. I walked into one of the stalls and just cried my eyes out while I was twitching almost uncontrollably.

I went home that day but couldn't stop thinking about the incident. It was an intense sexual experience for me and I wanted to see her again. I was terrified of losing her affection and I also wanted to fit in.

The next day, I approached her and said, "Do you want to go back into the woods with me? I promise things will be different."

She didn't say anything but just laughed out loud, and walked away.

I was horrified and still thought of her often during the next couple of weeks until summer reached its conclusion. We didn't talk during that time but I kept trying to think of ways to get her to like me again. I decided on the night before the last day of camp that I would try to talk to her again.

The next day, I followed her to her car and she must have noticed.

"What do you want, Steve?"

"Nothing."

"Obviously, you do. You have been staring at me the last few weeks so just say what you have to say because I would really like to leave."

I took a really big chance and said, "Sally, I miss you and I think I love you."

I really thought I was in love with her. I thought about her all the time and couldn't imagine not keeping in touch with her somehow during the school year.

"You can't fall in love with me. It's impossible. Nobody loves me. You're just fixated."

"I want to keep seeing you during the year."

"I'm not coming back here again, Steve. I'm not contacting you either."

I cried and began begging her to change her mind.

"I will change for you," I said with a desperation that was obviously a turn-off.

But, it was pointless and pathetic. Her mind was set and I couldn't change it.

"I have a boyfriend!" she cried out.

"I need you."

"You need some serious help. Steve, you know nothing about me."

"I know enough," I was reaching out for anything to keep her in my life, even for a few minutes longer. Perhaps she was right. Perhaps I was not in love and maybe I didn't understand my feelings at the time. I was overwhelmed by the intensity of the emotions and felt very scared. I was horrified that I was losing Sally.

"There is something missing with you and I am not going to stick around and find out more."

I thought that was awfully cold, even though it was probably best in the long run.

I began to cry even stronger again as I felt seriously wounded like a shot to the chest. My heart felt weak, and my nose was crinkling again. So I did what I was best at, which was to run away again. I made a dash for the bathroom so no one would see me crying. Even though it was the last day, I felt a need to keep my facade intact.

A few months later, during my senior year of high school, while thinking off and on about Sally, I received a letter from the director of the camp. It said that though I had been a loyal camper and counselor for a long period, he couldn't offer me a job this upcoming summer due to low enrollment. I felt horrible for two reasons. One being, that I would never see Sally or any of my summer friends again. The second was that I had failed at one more thing. I felt the urge to know more about why I had been fired.

My mother had known the director for years. Apparently, they had been to high school together and that was a large part of the reason I had been there so long. I thought I would give my mother a chance to see if she could help.

"Mom, I was fired from camp. They don't want me back according to this letter."

"How can that be?" she asked. She quickly came up to me and took the letter out of my hand.

She read the letter to herself a few times and just paused for a few seconds.

"What do you think, Mom?"

"I think you should call Lou and ask him for more details. This seems odd. They love you at that camp. You've done a great job for them."

I was touched that my mom was becoming more supportive of me.

"Can you call, Mom?"

"Steve, you are entering college next fall. You need to be able to talk to him."

"I'm scared."

"I know you are but part of growing up is being able to do things that you couldn't do as a child."

"Maybe I should ask Dad to call?"

My mom became agitated, "You always seek him out when you want to do things the easy way. Don't do that, Steve. Be strong and take my advice. I love you as well, Steve."

"I know but you're always so tough on me."

"The world is a scary place and you need to get tough."

That line stayed with me for a lifetime. The world was indeed "scary," at least for me who wasn't as well-adjusted as some of those handsome, confident boys in my high school.

I did call right away as my mom seemed supportive of me.

"Lou, this is Steve Goldberg."

"Hi Steve, I guess you are calling about the letter."

"Yes," I crinkled my nose as my mother watched me a few feet away.

"Steve, you've been a part of this camp a long time but we have seen attendance in the camp drop and so I had to let some people go. Everyone likes you but I'm sorry," he seemed like he wanted to say more but was fumbling for the right words. As for myself, I was very anxious as I wanted to find out the truth which I did not feel like I was getting.

"Lou, why am I being let go?"

"Steve, I spoke to some of your supervisors over the last few summers and they all seemed to agree that you are not quick enough for the job."

"I don't understand," I said, though I was having flashbacks of all the rituals I was consumed with, even in a place I liked. I could remember being late bringing the campers' lunches to the cafeteria because I had to stop in the bathroom every few steps to wash my hands. So I did know exactly what he was talking about.

"We just need quicker counselors, Steve. I'm sorry if that hurts."

It did hurt but he had a job to do, and taking my feelings and how they would affect me the rest of my life was not of concern to him.

I hung up the phone and stared at my mother who held her arms wide open for me to come and hug.

"What happened?" she asked quietly but with affection.

I was crying in my mom's arms now like a little child. I told her what the director had told me.

"He shouldn't have said that to you, Steve."

"Why not? It's the truth."

"He had no right to say you weren't quick enough. That can really damage a young person's self-esteem."

Little did she know how fragile my self-esteem already was, or perhaps she more aware of the situation than I gave her credit for. Either way, the discussion with Lou just made me think less of myself.

"Thanks for supporting me, Mom. I do love you."

"I know you do."

I disengaged from her warm arms and walked back to my room, this time wondering if Sally had said something to the director. I knew it was a long shot but maybe she called him after the last day and told him that I was not all there. But, she said she wasn't coming back so why would she drag me down with her? It didn't seem likely but it did seem possible. I thought about it for the next few weeks but soon my thoughts wandered toward my future as I was anxious to get out of the area. There was nothing here for me in New York anymore.

September 1991 to May 1995 – The College Years

My father dropped me off at the university and said, "If things don't go well, you can always come home."

I literally thought my family had bets on how long I would remain at college. For either academic or social reasons, they believed I wouldn't be able to make it work. However, as soon as I arrived, positive things started happening. My roommate John and I hit it off. We became quick friends. It was obvious that he was more socially adept than myself but for some reason, he seemed to accept me. We would study very much during the week, but we would also get pretty drunk on the weekends. We would sometimes, somehow, persuade a couple of girls to come to our room, and we would drink while watching movies. When I was drunk, I was a completely different person. My inhibitions left me and my true desires became evident.

One drunken night, I remembered something my mom told me the prior summer. She said that I should be careful when I'm with girls who have been drinking. She claimed they would tell me how much they liked me at night, but yell "rape," the following morning. This warning was similar to the conversation we had when I was seven, but it still struck a chord in me. She saw me as a nice, shy boy who could easily be manipulated. Regardless, one Friday night, I found myself playing drinking games with John and two cute coeds. I was interested in Jane who was blonde with curly hair. I thought she was flirting with me so I asked her if she wanted to walk with me. I only did that because John had told me weeks earlier that girls liked lines like that. She said yes and we made our way to a lounge in the dorm. She sat next to me and I told her how beautiful she was. That was my line. I always told girls from the time I was in the woods with Lisa that they were beautiful. I wasn't sure what to talk about and they seemed to like hearing how attracted I was to them. She turned toward me and we started kissing. Everything was going well but I couldn't get the conversation with my mom about rape out of my head.

"Are you drunk?" I asked.

"Just a little bit."

"I don't want you to do anything if you're drunk."

She put her hands over my mouth and said, "Relax."

We kissed some more as I felt myself oddly aroused with a woman for the first time. I was too scared of my mom's speech to have sex with her.

The following weekend, Jane and I went to a party together. We had a couple of beers and soon headed back to my dorm. John was away for the weekend so I knew I had exclusive use of the room. We sat on the bed and she leaned in to kiss me. I wanted to touch her but the vision of my mom lecturing to me about rape kept popping up in my brain.

"Stop, I have a question," I said nervously.

"I know what it is."

"What?" I said, though fearing that she had figured me out.

"I'm not drunk."

"Are you sure?"

"Yes, I'm sure."

"So you want to do this?" I asked.

"Yes," she replied but I still didn't feel reassured.

"I'm still not certain this is right," I really wanted to kiss her, to touch her, to allow myself free reign with her body. However, my fears and inhibitions kept crying out to me in my mind. I didn't want to disappoint myself, God, or my mother.

Jane looked upset as her face tensed up and became redder… "If we're going to have to go through this every time we go out, then it's just not worth it to me. I think I'm going to leave."

She left and I cried alone in my room. During the next few years, I would see Jane occasionally at nearby bars. No matter how drunk I would become, I never had the nerve to speak to her again.

During the spring of my freshman year, John and I pledged a fraternity. I thought it would be a great experience since booze and women were always available. Still, my compulsions wouldn't let go of me. Right before the end of the semester, at one of our fraternity parties, a sexy girl named Julie asked me abruptly if there was somewhere quiet we could go. I was very drunk and the house was mostly dark so I can't really recall what she was wearing or much of what was said. I wasn't even aware of what color hair she had, but there was definitely a feeling of sexiness about her. I took her to an empty bedroom upstairs and in no time, things were going further for me than I expected. Our clothes were off in no time and my hands were all over her naked body, caressing her breasts while I kissed her mouth. Her breath smelled a bit of alcohol, but mine probably did as well. I didn't really care and I was becoming more forceful with her as I pulled her breasts toward my lips. Her chest smelled like lavender or some sort of cheap bottled lotion from a Victoria's Secret. I wanted to go further with this girl as I was feeling very excited. I think she was really drunk, and horny for me as well. There was something stopping me. I saw my mother's face flash in my head and nervously asked, "Are things going too quickly?"

She then immediately pulled away, claiming, "Maybe things are going a little too fast, but I definitely want to get to know you better." I felt disappointed and relieved at the same time.

"I'm sorry," I said but she didn't respond as I could make out from the weak lighting in the room that she was getting dressed.

"I'm sorry," I repeated.

"You have nothing to be sorry about, sweetie." I had a good time. Too much, I think.

She came toward me, kissed me on the cheek, and left me a note with her phone number in my hands. I was angry at myself as I knew I could have had sex but I gave her too much time to think about it. I was drunk and confused. Maybe, it was better that my first time did not happen like that, I thought.

When summer arrived, I went back home to New York. I received my grades and for the second straight semester, I made the dean's list. I sat around the house all day watching episodes of Montel Williams, but my mind started to play tricks on me. The episode with Julie was gnawing at me. Maybe she was too drunk. Possibly, I took advantage of her. What if she told the cops and they were waiting for me at the start of my sophomore year? Only my mother was able to see the strain on me. I told her it was private and I couldn't talk to her regarding this matter. She insisted I communicate with someone so I scheduled an appointment with a social worker. Her name was Susan and I spoke about all my problems with her. She said something to me that would forever change my life.

"I think you have obsessive-compulsive disorder. Your mind confuses and fixates on things. For example, what your mother said about drunk girls could be true. For most of your peers, it would just be a word of caution. However, you fixated and fixated on it." That sentence by Susan completely rang true for me as I was forced to endure the effects of my mom's warning every night.

I saw Susan for the rest of the summer, but it did not alleviate my fears that I could have raped that girl. In the front of my mind, I knew that no actual intercourse had taken place. But, I was a drunken mess that night and maybe I was remembering things incorrectly. She said things could get worse, and if so, I should see a school psychiatrist for medication.

That particular summer, my thoughts were acting up something fierce. No matter how many times I talked to Susan, she could not ease my fear of being arrested when I got back to college.

"Why do you think you will be arrested?" she asked, the day before I was to be brought back to college by my dad.

"You know why."

"I want to hear you say it." I knew full well what she was getting at as I fumbled for the right words.

"I may have raped that girl."

"Do you really think, Steve, that you raped her, or is this just your mind fixating on your fears?"

"Probably the latter, but I am terrified she told her father about me and they went to the police and are waiting for me to check into my dorm to arrest me."

"Steve, that is not how the police work."

"How do you know?"

"They would have contacted you by now if there was an allegation."

The truth is that I didn't know how the police worked, but my fears were getting the worst of me.

"The poor girl didn't know where I lived and she is from Texas so it just might be easier for the cops to wait for me to check in to my dorm."

"Then what?" she replied. "The cops are going to be summoned to your dorm. This is not making sense, Steve, and this is not going to happen."

"How do you know?"

"Steve, you were drunk that night, right?"

"Very much."

"And I've seen kids your age steal cars and get into all kinds of trouble while inebriated and nothing that you're imagining happened."

"I'm still scared," I said. I felt at that point comforted by the therapist as it seemed like she had some experience in dealing with people my age. I just wasn't sure if she could completely heal me and bring my mind to a state of peace. Because, at that point, my mind was racing a million miles a minute.

"You are going to continue to be scared until you realize how bad this OCD is for you and that the drinking can exacerbate it."

I knew she was correct but I didn't know if I could give up drinking. I loved alcohol and how it made me feel. It gave me courage though I knew I was still just a scared boy. Of course, I hated the ramifications the next morning when I was unsure what happened.

"I drink only on weekends because I need relief from all my thoughts when I'm at school. A break from all my washings and rituals."

"Steve, the way you're living through is not healthy and it is not helping your obsessive thoughts."

I thought to myself, *what did this nice young woman know about stress and obsessive thoughts?* From the corner of my eye, I could see the picture of her and her husband on their wedding day. She had everything and I had nothing. Nothing.

"Maybe I should just stay away from girls at this point in my life."

"You are 19, with raging hormones. Do you really think that is possible?"

"I'm not sure."

"I'm sure of the following, Steve, and that is getting drunk at frat parties and fooling around with strangers is dangerous for you."

I was confused by what she was telling me. Did she want me to give up girls?

"So you are saying I should stay away from girls right now?"

"No, I'm saying that you should try to meet a girl in a sober environment. It would be better for your state of mind."

"But Susan, my symptoms would still flare up."

"Yes, they would, but it wouldn't be as long-lasting and as detrimental as situations like these. Steve, I'm telling you this for your own benefit."

"What?" I was becoming more curious as to where she was leading because I did not like the idea of giving up drinking as it was my favorite escape. I had nothing else to turn to.

"Steve, you are a good-looking young man and if you put yourself out there, whether sober or drunk, you are going to find plenty of girls that are interested."

I was wondering why she was telling me this. At best, maybe I was average looking but the girls in high school never seemed interested, so it was hard for me to believe that I could have a lot of choices. It seemed easier when I was drunk. I was the outgoing person I was at camp when I got hammered at school. It seemed to me that the girls from high school and the girls I hooked up with in camp and college did not have the same image of me. Was I two different people? Who the fuck was I?

"Maybe, Susan, but it just seems so much easier for me when I'm drunk."

"So I take it you are going to continue drinking and self-medicating when you get back tomorrow?"

"Most likely," I felt ashamed.

"Then you really don't want my help, do you?"

"I want you to help alleviate my thoughts from my OCD but not curb my drinking." I must have raised my voice because she raised hers as well.

"Steve, they go hand in hand. One affects the other. Why can't you see that?" She scared me a little bit as I was never good with confrontations.

"I see it, Susan," I said, lowering my voice. "I just fail to believe that my disorder will go away if I stop drinking."

"It won't, Steve, but the aftermath that you suffer the following days wondering if you harmed anyone will lessen."

"I agree, Susan. I'm just…"

"What?"

"I'm scared," I finally said.

"I know you are."

"Do you know what I'm scared of?" I asked.

"I think so."

"I'm terrified of living with the pain of being myself."

"Do you love yourself more when you are inebriated, Steve?"

I paused but I knew the answer, "I think everyone loves me more when I drink." Even when I told her that, I was lying a little bit because the truth was that I liked myself more as well when I drank.

Fall 1993

I did make it back to college that year and everything occurred as my therapist predicted. There were no charges pending against me when I checked into my dorm room. The cops were not waiting for me. The weeks went on and I continued to study hard during the week, binge drink on weekends, and fortunately make out with other drunk girls at the parties. Things went a little too far one Saturday night in October when I had become very inebriated during one of the parties. I was feeling excited and even somewhat horny but it was becoming increasingly obvious that I was not going to have any female companions that night as the festivities were winding down. I went all over the house which was three stories, looking for any female who would want to talk and hopefully fool around with me.

As luck would have it, one of my fraternity brother's girlfriends told me that her friend Lisa who was visiting from out of town wanted to meet me. I was told that she thought I was very cute. I met Lisa and though I could tell she had a pretty face, she was a little larger than what I preferred. However, as I downed beer after beer, she was looking more attractive. She also kept looking directly into my eyes. I was beyond fucked up and thought this might be my chance.

"Is there somewhere we can go to talk more?" she asked when she approached me.

"You bet," I said, as I dragged her hand up the staircase.

I knew there was an empty bedroom upstairs so I led her to the room and locked the door for privacy.

"Do you want to turn on the television?"

"Sure," I said as she quickly took a seat on the bed.

I don't recall everything that happened next, but I vaguely remember putting my arm around her and leaning in to kiss her. She was from out of town and seemed like she had been around the block a few times. She was very aggressive with her words which led me to being shocked when she moved away from my attempt to kiss her on the lips.

"Not yet," she whispered.

I must have felt confused so I put my hand on her chest and she yanked it away. She then got up off the bed and I lunged with my hands forward toward her chest and she said adamantly, "No, stop, Steve."

"What's a matter?" I managed to say. "I want to kiss you."

My speech had begun to slur and she said, "You are too wasted. I've changed my mind."

I suddenly felt betrayed. I was excited and she had given me every signal that something would happen.

"But you asked to come and be alone with me. I thought this is what you wanted."

"I thought so too but I'm not comfortable now and I would like to leave."

"You are free to leave. You just shouldn't have gotten me all worked up."

I was standing away from the door, allowing her the ability to leave the room but for some reason, she stayed for a few seconds. I then started to cry. I was overwhelmed with angst and confusion. I was pissed at the girl, but also furious at myself for allowing myself to lose control.

"Should I get some help?" she asked.

"I'm sorry. I'm sorry I touched you. I didn't mean it," I said, bawling into the pillow as I lay down on my bed.

"You were wrong, Steve. You seem like a decent guy but I just don't want to hook up tonight. I'm sorry about the confusion."

My disorder along with the alcohol was really starting to turn things into a higher gear as I asked her more inappropriate questions.

"Are you going to turn me in to the police?" my tears were covering the pillow.

"What are you talking about?" she seemed puzzled.

"Are you going to have me arrested?"

"No," she said a little loudly as I became alarmed that someone might hear us. There were people drinking in a room about two doors down with some music playing.

"You don't want to send me to jail?" I knew I was losing control of my thoughts and speech but I desperately needed confirmation I was not going to go to prison for rape.

"No, I just want to leave this room and the house."

She must have been an awfully nice person though I didn't realize it at the time. She said, "Steve, why don't you go to the bathroom and clean yourself up?"

I got up and was still crying. "I'm sorry," I said to her repeatedly as I made my way to the bathroom.

Only about a minute passed before I heard a knock on the door. I finally became aware that Lisa must have told someone because when I opened the door, my roommate John walked in to see me.

"Are you okay?"

"No."

"You look like you've been crying. Everyone's leaving including Lisa."

"Is she going to the police station?"

"You need help, Steve."

I knew as usual, John was right.

"I'm fine."

I was the opposite of fine but I was trying to maintain some composure.

"She just said you tried to kiss her and she moved, so you got upset. Did anything else happen?"

"No."

"Let's go back to the dorm and we will talk about this tomorrow."

I went back to the dorm room with John but felt horrible. Who was I? What made me so aggressive with that nice girl and why did I get so upset? I knew then that I needed to follow my therapist's advice and stop drinking. I did not need a woman crying rape ever again. I vaguely remember crying myself to sleep in the fetal position.

The next morning I informed John about my intention to stop drinking. I was also going to call my father for moral support. My father never drank, but I did not know the reason behind his decision. *Maybe*, I thought, *he can help explain them to me and listen to my concerns.* He was always there for me and it had been several weeks since I called home. I was worried about how much detail involving last night's incident I should give out, but after all, he was my dad. I was feeling so ashamed as I knew my mom with her strict moral code would judge me and I also felt that God was shaking his head down on me.

I picked up the phone and went for it.

"Dad, I went too far last night."

"With what, son?"

"Dad, please don't tell Mom anything I disclose to you."

"I will try not to but what is this about? Besides, Mom is out shopping."

"I think I went too far with a girl last night."

"Good for you, Steve."

"No, Dad, this is not a good thing," I took a deep breath and tried to navigate my way through the conversation.

"You got laid, son. It's okay to have mixed feelings but…"

He obviously was not understanding me and I resented his cavalier attitude about sex. I thought maybe if he had spoken to me about girls when I was living at home, I would be having fewer problems. But I also knew I was looking for someone to blame, besides myself.

"Dad, I did not get laid but I tried to force myself on some girl."

I couldn't believe I said that so clearly since it was probably an odd thing for a father to hear about his son.

"What exactly happened, Steve? Your mom tried to talk to you before you left for college about alcohol and rape."

"I don't think I raped her."

"Were you drunk?"

"I was very inebriated."

"What happened, Steve? I'm concerned by the way you're speaking that you are in trouble."

"I'm not in trouble."

"Did you rape someone, Steve?" *Did he really think I could do that*, I thought to myself. Again, who the fuck was I? I was not the shy boy from my high school any longer.

"Of course not."

"I knew you were not capable of that, son."

My mind was racing back and forth trying to think of the events of last night. It was 11 am and I was sober but did I accurately remember the events? I was worried that maybe something darker happened than I remembered.

"Dad, I didn't rape this girl but I was very intoxicated and I got touchy with her."

"You grabbed her without her permission?"

"Yes, Dad."

"Is that all?"

"Yes, I lost control of my impulses. I thought she wanted something to happen, but she withdrew and I lunged after her a few times until I just started sobbing." My words were becoming increasingly louder and more intense as if I had to draw a picture to my dad about what went on.

"So there was no sex of any kind, Steve?" My dad's voice was calm but he was more inquisitive than usual. Perhaps I had hit a sensitive subject.

"No." At least 99% of my brain was telling me that the way I remembered it was correct but it was that 1% of my disorder that was trying to trick me into thinking that more had happened. I knew I had to listen to the rational side because I didn't even know how to have sex. I had no memory of either me or that poor girl with our clothes off.

"So you grabbed her a bit, Steve, and then when she refused, in your drunken mess, you started crying."

"Yes, Dad. That is all that happened," I felt tears come out of my eyes and my voice got scratchy as it always did when I started to sob.

"It's going to be all right son. You just have to stop drinking."

"I want to, but it helps me."

"Steve, listen to me. Maybe for a brief time, it helps alleviate some of your stress, but it leads to more problems like last night." He sounded like my therapist and I was growing tired of these easy solutions.

"I'm not an animal, Dad," though I wasn't quite sure who or what I was becoming.

"Who says you are? You are a good person. You just made a mistake. Did you apologize to the girl?" His voice was sounding more reassuring and less interrogative.

"Yes, and she seemed very understanding. She was visiting from another college and I thought she liked me and then when…" I continued to cry into the phone. "Dad, help me. My mind is running wild."

"It's all right, son. Your judgment was impaired and you misread the signals."

"Dad, what if I had done more to her?"

"But you are telling me you didn't."

"I know, but I'm scared that I'm remembering the events wrong."

"It's just your illness hitting you in your weak spots, Steve. What you remember is what happened. Don't make it into something that your mind is trying to trick you into believing. Fight this monster."

"I don't know that I can do it alone," I felt like an extremely weak person. I was not a strong, healthy person like my older brother. I wish I was him.

"I'll do whatever I can to help you, Steve."

"I want to speak to my social worker about my drinking."

"Steve, take the train home this weekend, and then I will drive you back to school Sunday night. In the meantime, you can schedule an appointment with her for Saturday. She will see you."

I was relieved that I was able to have this conversation with my loving father and not my mother. I know she loved me but she was just so darn strict. Also, it would be good to see the therapist and take a weekend off from partying.

"Are you okay, son, or do you need me to come to visit you now?"

"No, John is watching over me and I feel better."

"You sure you don't want me to swing by?"

"No, it will only alarm Mom."

"Your mother would give up her own life for you, Stevie. One day you will understand the depth of her love."

"Dad," I said quietly, as my tears had dried up and my voice was back to normal, "why don't you drink?" My hands shook a bit as I knew I was asking for something sensitive.

"Come home, son." He did not want to give an answer. Maybe it would have pained him too much to answer or maybe it would have hurt me to hear the truth about my father.

I entered Susan's office on Saturday morning, relieved and anxious at the same time. Relieved because I would finally be able to get the help I needed, and anxious because I was nervous about how far I had fallen. I was also a little nervous about how Susan would react to my episode. When I finished relaying the tale to her, she asked me a serious question.

"What do you want from me, Steve?"

She seemed fed up with me.

I was a little puzzled by the question because my presence alone should have indicated to her that I was serious about quitting drinking.

"I'm done with alcohol," I quietly stated, a little taken aback by the question.

"Is that what you really want?"

"Why do you ask? Why else would I be here?" I felt agitated as if she was mocking me.

"Well, clearly you are a little bit shaken up by what happened, but you told me over the summer that you need alcohol to ease the pain, as a way of self-medicating."

"So?" I said, still not clearly grasping where she was going with this.

"Steve, if you want to give up alcohol, you will have to confront your demons sober and that can be a very frightening thing for anyone, especially you."

"I thought I was coming here for help, so why are you lecturing me?" I was growing annoyed and a little resentful that she was not acknowledging me for taking the initial steps toward recovery. I believe she doubted my sincerity.

"I just want to make sure that you are not just going through a passing phase and then start drinking again."

"What phase? What are you talking about?" my voice got a little louder as I was growing confused.

"No need to get upset. I just want to make sure that you are serious about remaining sober. Sometimes, young adults get shaken up by an incident, but then realize that it is easier to drink than face their own issues."

"In all seriousness, I think that is a little too much over analysis as your people would call it."

"I'm glad you think so because I warned you this summer that alcohol and your condition was a bad mixture."

I knew she was right and that kept me coming back to her.

"I should have listened but I don't think I was ready to."

"Unfortunately, it took an incident that frightened you to realize there had to be a better way to deal with your OCD."

The tone of her voice had become more soothing so I thought I could begin to let my defenses down.

"I think it's fortunate that this incident wasn't worse, but I'm still scared."

"Of what, Steve?"

My hands were starting to tremble but I continued in a slower, softer, more deliberate manner, "I'm terrified that I could be a rapist. Do you think I could be a rapist?"

"Don't look at me for reassurance. I'm curious about what you think."

"Can you please just answer the question? I need to know."

"Again, it sounds like you are looking for me to reassure you, but that won't help you with your disorder, your drinking, or your relationships."

There was an awkward moment of silence where we both didn't say anything. I felt like she really had a handle on my disorder and was able to figure me out in a way my mother never could. Of course, I could never talk to my mother about sex and females.

Finally, she asked, "Why are you afraid you might be some sort of rapist?"

"I'm just wondering if I was left alone with a woman and my anger was out of control while I was drinking, would I rape someone?"

"But to the best of your knowledge, have you ever raped anyone?"

"No."

"So, there is your answer."

I was angry at her for not just telling me. "No, Steve, you are not a rapist." That is what I wanted to hear, but she wouldn't give in to my mind's need for constant reassurance. She was very strong and very clever.

"But if I continue to drink, I'm scared something like rape could happen."

"Then, there is your answer. Don't drink. Alcohol fuels your anger and makes you misperceive situations with girls. Then, in the morning, your OCD makes your mind wander and wander, into unchartered territories."

She totally got me.

"Well, I want to stop drinking. And I came back to see you because I thought you could help."

"I think I can too, but the desire and the actions are going to have to come from you."

I felt much calmer talking with her in the office as I realized I had never raped anyone, but I had to get a handle on my drinking to make sure I never would.

"Susan, do you know why I want to stop drinking?"

"Yes, but I want to hear you tell me. I'm not going to tell you everything."

"It's that I am more scared, for the first time, of drinking than not drinking."

"Can you expand on that, Steve?"

"Well, for what seems like the longest time, I was so scared of not drinking because I did not want to deal with the pain of facing my issues. It was easier to just keep drinking until I passed out. But now, I'm terrified of what could happen from my actions when I'm drunk. It seems all my inhibitions wash away and I don't want to become that madman that I was the other night."

My hands started to fidget momentarily as I thought back on that helpless coed whom I preyed upon. My voice started to crack again just like it did when I was a scared grade-school student. Then, as always, the tears came. It seemed like for a solid five minutes I was sobbing and doing so loudly.

Susan watched me sob from her seat, shaking her head sideways in disbelief. I wanted her to hug me but knew that was not a possibility. Yet, I wanted to find someone like her that understood me.

I went back to the university that following Monday and let my brothers know that I would not be drinking anymore. I was quitting cold turkey. It was too painful to drink and I figured it would be smooth sailing for the rest of my academic career. However, I soon realized that my OCD would attack everything I loved, targeting all my weaknesses. Academics was something I valued and for the duration of my college career, would be something that my disorder would deviously take advantage of.

It started in one of my entry-level psychology classes run by Dr. Stringer. I can't really explain the processes of how it happened, but the OCD found a way to infect my presence in his classroom.

I would sit quietly in the packed auditorium and felt myself, just like in high school, the need to curse out loud or at least mutter something. Dr. Stringer was a white male so it wasn't a racial epithet that I was scared of voicing, but just evil words. For instance, I had to fight every desire not to say, "Dr. Stringer, I will kill you." Back then, my fear wasn't of going to jail but that if my professor read my lips, he would give me an F. Then, I would have to go back home and flip burgers.

The way my mind worked was that he would read my lips, and wait until the end of the summer to exact his revenge. He would come across my file when grading his students and would flunk me. This would in turn hurt my chances of graduating and even possibly put me on academic probation. In addition, he might look into my schedule and contact my other professors to let them in on what I was saying in class, and then all my professors would fail me sending me back home for the rest of my life. I was nothing and I would amount to nothing.

This made me want to drink at the parties but I was able to resist because I did not want to turn into the rapist-monster that I was capable of becoming. My life had become twisted and almost unbearable.

When I returned home for a break after finals, I was terrified of receiving my grades even though I knew I aced my exams. Even when the mail finally came with my report card showing straight A's, things still went haywire. I thought my obsession with Dr. Stringer would be over, but he unknowingly was an active part of my life. If only the doctor knew he was terrorizing me.

Every day, while watching TV alone in my family room, I started to think that Dr. Stringer was watching me from outside the windows. So every five minutes, I would think I said, "Dr. Stringer, I will kill you," and then have to go upstairs, through the door, into the backyard and search in the trees for Dr. Stringer. This was all due to my need to reassure myself that he was not there. Even though the best part of my mind knew he wasn't really there, I couldn't help myself. My mind was growing weaker and my joy of life was eroding. I rarely asked myself what I would say if I did see my professor. He was in a position of authority and I wasn't. However twisted I had become, I knew that I feared anyone who could control my life. And these professors could dictate whether you worked in a fast-food restaurant or go on to law school.

I did not enjoy living anymore. It was a horrid existence as I imagined my life crumbling to pieces. If my professor failed me and I was forced to work some menial job, I would also say things to my boss there. I would then get fired from my job and just be a burden on my parents, particularly my mother.

My parents and brothers were out of the house during the break so I was able to keep up with my rituals. I was constantly running into the backyard to look for the educated professor who had nothing better to do with his time than watch me say threatening things. It was funny but sadder, at the same time.

I thought about drinking, just so I could pass out and not have to deal with my life. I was scared to live and scared to die. Suicide was not an option for me. I would never be so selfish as to end my life and leave my dad in a state of despair. They deserved better, even my mom who started to be nicer to me and ask me questions.

I think she must have noticed how unhappy I was because one morning when she and I were the only ones up, she asked me a startling question.

"Has anyone touched you, Steve?"

I was tired but like a quick B-vitamin shot, I was made quickly aware of the nature of the conversation.

"No."

"Has anyone at school touched you without your permission?" she repeated.

"Mom, I appreciate your concern but the answer is still no."

"It's just that you seem so unhappy, worse than usual."

"Thanks," I said, as my sarcasm remained intact.

"Steve, I know you are closer with your dad which is okay with me, but I need you to know that I love you too."

I was surprised that my mom was speaking to me so sensitively. I wasn't sure how to handle it.

"Thanks, Mom, I love you too but I'm not sure I'm good enough to be your son."

"Where do you get these ideas from?" she looked puzzled.

"Dad gets me, Mom, but I don't think you truly, after all this time, understand what makes me tick."

"Help me understand, Steve."

It occurred to me at that second that maybe I didn't understand my mom at all. We could tell each other a hundred times that we loved one another but I don't know if we really liked one another. Nobody ever wonders that. Family members tell each other all the time that they love one another, but do they really enjoy their company? I could hang out with my dad for hours watching a Yankee game but my mom, what did I really have in common with her other than blood?

"Well, Steve, what makes you tick?"

"I shouldn't have to tell you, Mom. You should know."

"Steve, have I been so terrible a mother that you think I don't care for you? I know I'm impatient but I do the best I can with what I have." At this point, she seemed flustered like a second-grader not getting their way.

"It just seems like you prefer my brothers," knowing that statement alone could cause an uproar.

"They are easier but that doesn't mean I don't care about you."

I was infuriated. How can she say they were easier than me? I mean, yes, they were but were they as dedicated to my dad as I was?

I silenced her quickly, "Mom, I don't want to hear it because actions speak louder than words and your actions suck."

I was shocked at my behavior and the amount of built-up anger that I still had after all this time toward the woman who gave birth to me.

"Don't talk to me like that, Steve. I love you too much to deserve this right now."

She looked like she was starting to have tears come down her face and I was left for once, speechless.

She must have not known either what to say next, because out of habit, she started screaming, "Bob, Bob, come down quickly and speak to your boy."

When my kind dad got there, he asked, "What is going on here?"

"There is nothing to talk about."

"Then, why all the commotion?"

"I don't know," I said while eyeballing my mother until I turned my back on both of them.

He and my mom let me walk away, and I did what I always did best: run, hide, and cry.

When I returned to my room, I was sobbing. I was forced to wonder what I did to deserve such a wretched existence. Why was God punishing me?

I thought about calling Rabbi Feldman, my mean rabbi who said he would always be there for me throughout my life.

A few minutes later, impulsively, I called the synagogue and asked the receptionist to put me through to Rabbi Feldman. She said that he was on another call but that he would definitely get in touch with me… I waited for a few days and still did not hear anything.

I called again and this time the receptionist asked if I wanted his voicemail. My message might have seemed somewhat scary to the rabbi who lived in a seemingly perfect world but he was a man of God. I needed answers as to why God was punishing me and I didn't think my therapist could help me with such complex issues. My message said something to the effect of "Hi, Rabbi Feldman, it's me, Steve Goldberg and I am in dire need of your assistance. I have been afflicted with a horrible mental disorder and would like your advice on how to get my life back on track and in accordance with God."

He never called me back. I often wondered why, but I realized that my intuition was correct. He lived in a perfect world and did not need any disruptions. He did not need any aggravation when I was a child and did not appreciate my intruding into his peaceful world, now as an adult. I just don't understand how a man could tell me that he would always be my spiritual leader, and then ignore me. I thought I would speak to my father who was a practicing Jew and always had the correct answers for me, even though I thought this was over his head.

"Dad, do you believe Jews are the chosen people as Rabbi Feldman used to say?"

"I'm not sure."

"Well, what do you believe in?"

"Steve, why are you asking me these questions? What matters is what you believe."

"I believe God is punishing me for being a bad person and even Rabbi Feldman won't help me."

"No one is punishing you and leave the rabbi out of this. He is and always was an asshole."

I was shocked that my father was being so candid with me, but it caused me to chuckle. My dad always knew what to say and the timing was always perfect. He was quite a mensch.

"Why, Dad, didn't you tell me that years ago?"

"I was just trying to get you to have a Bar Mitzvah, and so I tolerated him. I need to know what is going on because your mom and I are very concerned."

"The bottom line is, Dad, that I just don't enjoy living anymore."

He looked stunned as if I told him his mom had been heinously murdered.

"What are you saying?"

"Nothing, I'm not going to kill myself so you don't have anything to worry about."

"I love you, Steve. You're my little tiger and it hurts me to hear you talk like this."

"I'll work through it, Daddy."

"Do you want to take some time off from school and get help?"

"There is no help for me because there is no one like me."

I was so caught up in my own world that I was too self-absorbed to realize the suffering I was causing.

"You are so wrong, little tiger. We can get help for you. Why don't you give that nice social worker a call and see if she can help?"

"This is beyond her."

"What exactly is going on? Because you were able to stop drinking when alcohol was affecting your life. Maybe you just need some time to address these issues."

"I don't need time because my OCD targets all my hopes and dreams. It's slowly killing me."

"What exactly is going on?"

"I don't really want to go into it but to be brief, I feel out of control and my professors are in our backyard conspiring against me."

"I need to get you help, Steve," he said, with much austerity.

"They're trying to flunk me in my classes."

"There is nobody outside and you did well in all your classes." I appreciated his attempts at reassurance but knew it was a lost cause. I was too far gone to be helped.

"I know there really is no one outside but I keep having doubts so I constantly go out of the house to check the yard and make sure no one is there."

"So you have trouble with the constant doubting," he said, as he started to tear up and bury his head in his hands.

"Don't cry, Dad."

"How could I not? I love you and you are clearly suffering. It would mean everything to your mother and me if you at least gave the therapist a chance in the next week before you return to college."

"Hey Dad, I never doubted your love for me."

He was still crying and then said something inaudible. I asked him to cheer up because I would visit my social worker and make something out of my life. I didn't want him to give up hope, as that is all he seemed to have at the moment.

"Steve, you know what they call OCD in France, right?"

"Tell me."

The tears seemed to dry up for this strong man and he seemed more relaxed.

He said, "The Doubting Disease."

Two days later, I entered my therapist's office. She squeezed me into her schedule because I told her over the phone about how I thought I was under constant surveillance from my professors. She said she would do her best to help me.

"I'm sorry you are not doing well," she said compassionately as I entered her office.

She was a sweet woman but I was doubting whether any of this would work. I was starting to feel aches in my stomach as I just wanted to get out of there.

"Bottom line, can you help me?" I asked.

"I sincerely don't know but I think from what you have been telling me over the course of our working relationship, you should probably see a psychiatrist who specializes in treating OCD."

"So you think medicine will do the trick."

"No, but I think a combination of therapy and medicine could help. There are doctors I can refer you to."

It seemed to me then that she was bowing out gracefully as the limits of her position and knowledge had been stretched to the limits.

"I want to go back to school and finish my degree, no matter how painful and twisted that sounds."

"Well, Steve, there are doctors probably at the college that can prescribe medicine to you but do you really think it's a good idea to go right back this week? I mean, why don't you take a semester off and see if you can get help?"

I sensed that she was eager to help me and did not want me back at college, but school was an obsession too. I did not know what I wanted to do after I graduated but I felt a compelling, burning desire to go back and finish the next few years. It was what everyone in my Jewish town did, and what they expected.

"I only go to college a few hours away. Maybe I can see you every two or three weekends?"

"So you are going to go back," she said, shaking her head.

"I have to."

"Why?"

"I know it doesn't make sense but it's an obsession for me that I do well and finish up."

"Could I talk you out of this?"

"I don't think so," I said firmly.

I smiled at her, appreciating her help, but knowing there was no turning back for me.

"Well then, just know that you can call me any time, and I want you to see a psychiatrist at the school and they can call me as well, provided I have your consent."

"I will take care of it."

I knew I couldn't really take care of it but I was handed a bad deck of cards from God and I had to play this out.

"Steve, professors hear and see things in their classroom every day. They are not looking to get you and they are not watching you. You know that, right?"

"I think so, but I have to keep checking."

"This is no way to live," she said but she was grasping at straws. I had my mind made up. I would continue like everyone else that I knew and fit in as a college student.

Junior Year-1994

I still wasn't drinking and my behavior at parties was pretty laid back. Sure, I did not fool around with any girls being sober as I was too reluctant and scared where it would lead. Many of my fraternity brothers had even distanced themselves from me because I did not drink. John still stood by me but he didn't understand me completely because I was terrified to tell him about all my paranoia and rituals.

As for taking medication, I tried several but none of them seemed to work. After a while, I stopped going to the psychiatrists at the student health center. I did go home about once a month to talk with Susan but things were not improving and I sensed disappointment in her voice when we spoke.

It was the same thing each semester. I would be terrified that my professors were looking into my room and seeing me curse at them, perform the necessary checks to make sure they weren't there, and then get A's when the report cards came. I started to think that once I graduated, things would be better as school, I perceived, was the stimulus for most of my OCD. Surely, this was no way to live but the pain would be temporary and then life would get better.

I have to admit the checking was getting out of control so much so that I hated leaving my room. On walks to the library or class, every time I muttered something, I would have to turn around and make sure none of my professors were within hearing range. I would walk alone to and from wherever I needed to go and thought I was covering all my tracks and keeping my secrets intact until one evening John confronted me about my bizarre behavior.

"We need to talk, Steve. I saw you walking today from afar."

I was immediately terrified and felt my body clench up.

"What are you talking about, John? I have to study," I said, wanting to avoid the conversation.

"Can it, Steve," he said with great authority.

"I don't know what you are talking about."

"I saw you walking and it was downright scary. Why are you turning around every few seconds? You look like some freak."

I looked at his face and he looked scared, more terrified than I had ever seen him on any occasion.

"I don't wish to discuss this, John."

"I know but it looks like you are in a lot of pain."

"Again, I can't talk about it."

He understood me. I was in pain but I had to linger on. I had no choice.

"Maybe you should give me a chance," he said. His voice seemed calmer than initially, and he was coming across as empathetic. His demeanor had also changed as his face seemed untightened and eager to listen to me.

"I have a therapist," I continued.

"Maybe you need a friend."

"You're a great friend, John, but this is bigger than you would imagine."

"I know you are not well, Steve, so why not give me an opportunity to help you?"

It seemed like John genuinely wanted to help, but again, I was not willing to let someone who cared about me get ensnared in my warped world. Though I was touched by his kindness and I felt a bit like opening up, I knew I would never allow it.

"Let me take you out for dinner, Steve, and we will just talk—me and you."

I was sincerely tempted to take him up on this offer but I still felt something pulling me away.

"I appreciate your sincerity, John, but you would be entering a hellish world that you don't need to know about."

"But, I want to. I want to help and offer some kind of assistance."

"There is no help for people like me, John."

"What the fuck does that mean?" he raised his voice.

I was shocked. John went from calm and cool to pissed off. I guess he was used to getting his way.

"I'm suffering and I don't want to take you down with me," I could feel my voice crack as if I was about to cry.

"Stevie, haven't I always looked out for you. Don't you know that you are not going to bring me down? That I would never abandon you?"

"I know you wouldn't abandon me but I just can't let you into this place. Besides, you say that now, but once you see what kind of a snake we are dealing with, you may run for the hills."

I started my usual crying as I was touched by John but scared to go any further. This was a conversation usually reserved for my father.

"Stevie, you are going to have to trust someone one day, besides a therapist or doctor. People need friends, girls, and companions."

"I agree with all you are saying, John, but all I could tell you at this point is that after college, things will get better."

"Why would they get better?" he seemed confused.

"I can't explain, except that my symptoms are symptomatic of my experiences here and they will go away when I go home and enter the workforce."

"You really believe that?" he asked, as he chuckled a bit.

The truth is I wasn't sure what I believed. I figured that things would have to ease up on me after graduation for me to live an enjoyable life because there was no enjoyment here and there was no one else like me to confide in. Again, I just wanted to fit in, at least as long as I could keep this up without killing myself in the process. I could limp forward to graduation.

I became very pensive and started to think about what my home life would be like after 1995. However, I couldn't imagine anything right now; no family, job, or anything else. I couldn't think past today as I just wanted to make it to the finish line. I could feel John staring at me. I cared for him but I had chosen a course of battle that did not include his suffering.

"You believe that your life will be great after graduation?"

"John, it doesn't need to be great. I've never been a happy-go-lucky individual but I believe that it will be normal."

"Maybe you have to believe that to keep going," he said affirmatively.

He was the only friend who challenged me and he was right to a point. I did have to believe that things would be normal. I had been through a war in my young life and I knew if I could make it out of this place alive, things could only get better.

"Steve, I hope to stay in contact with you after college and let me know how things are going. I'm your brother and you can always count on me."

"I know this, John," I said, wiping the remaining tears away from my eyes.

"Somehow, I don't think you are going to include me in your life, Steve."

I definitely wanted to include him and hoped that once things returned to normal, we could talk on the phone and possibly visit, but I couldn't promise anything, honestly. And, of course, his skills at perception cut through me as I started to sob again. It was an awkward thing for one friend to say to another, but at least it was honest.

"Why would you say that, John? You are my best friend."

"I'm your only friend, Steve. Sorry, you are crying and I hate to be so cut and dry about it. But let's be honest, you've shut everyone out. God help you if you shut your immediate family out as well."

I was starting to feel angry as it was clear that this conversation was triggering me; I could feel the parts of my face, such as my nose, begin to twitch.

"That is none of your fuckin' business, John."

"To hell it's not."

"John, I don't want to fight with you so could you please back off a bit?"

"I will but under one condition. That you hug me."

I had tried to fight back my tears but I was genuinely touched. I asked myself what I had done to deserve such a friend as John.

"You don't need to cry, Stevie. I just want you to know I love you."

I continued to sob, "What does hugging me have to do with it?"

"I think you can use a hug right about now. Am I right?"

I felt a bit uneasy about hugging John. I had seen members of my fraternity give each other hugs but I had never been included. The fraternity was now just an organization that I belonged to that was comparable to a chess club. There was no brotherhood involved in it for me; except for John who I kept trying to keep out. Anyways, I was hesitant about hugging any male besides my father. As for my two brothers, we were not close so it never came up. I wanted him to know I cared about him but I didn't know how much further I could go.

"John, I don't do hugs with men."

"How is that working for you, Steve, pushing everyone who cares for you out of your life?"

"Not great."

"You know, it doesn't make you gay. You know, Steve, I'm the least gay guy around. I got laid first when I was 12."

"Good to know."

We both laughed as my tears had dried up.

"Well, Steve, can I get that hug?"

"Maybe sometime in the future, John. I just can't. I'm sorry."

I'm not sure why I couldn't, or if something happened to me as a child which failed to prepare me for male bonding. Anyways, I couldn't get past my uneasiness about the situation.

"Don't be sorry. You're the one who needs it, but I will wait until you are ready."

I knew for sure that I did need family and that I would never have as close a brother as John. He saw something in me that my own two brothers failed to see. I wanted to be the person he thought I was, not some schmuck that my two real brothers thought I was.

Senior Year

I would love to say that things changed for the better, but that was not the case. I was still performing my rituals and checking things day and night. However, I was passing my classes and graduation was now only a few months away. I was unsure of what would happen after college, but I sincerely thought that John would be wrong. I envisioned a life that would be far from perfect, but a distant cry from my now shattered existence.

I also was lonely and thought that once I graduated and adjusted to life, I could start meeting girls on the job or elsewhere. It had been a lonely few years since I successfully gave up drinking. I only succeeded at that, because I was so terrified of the alternative. I knew I had some game when it came to talking with the opposite sex, but without alcohol, my conversations were severely limited. But to be frank, I was horny and thought it was time for me to start trying to get some action. So, despite how warped my life was, I wanted some normalcy. Girlfriends or just one girl would help restore my life for the better. My goals were becoming clear. Get a job after graduation and start having sex. I knew I could do it without a problem, or at least I believed I could. I was determined to get my life back on track in the next month so that I could achieve my goals. That also meant cutting down on my obsessions involving my teachers. Women would not want to get to know me if they saw what John saw last year, and who knows, honestly, how many other people were witnesses to my downfall. Women only could love someone who they deemed as perfect or close to it.

I was determined to cut my rituals down but also realized I needed some practice talking with the opposite sex. I, therefore, scheduled a session for the weekend with my ever-loyal therapist, Susan.

"You said you had some good news for me, Steve," she said with a smile as I sat down in her office.

"I'm graduating and I have been practicing cutting down on my rituals."

"Which ones?"

"The ones where I keep looking for my professors hiding somewhere, looking for a reason to flunk me."

"Is it working?"

"Significantly."

"That's terrific, Steve, why do you think that is?"

"I'm feeling more at ease knowing I will graduate and this will be behind me."

She gave me a strange look as if I told her something so odd that she had never heard such a thing. I was puzzled by her weird stare at me and I knew I said something wrong.

"So you still think the OCD is just a part of college?"

"I'm proving that it is. I'm walking back from classes with more ease."

"Is it completely gone, Steve?"

"No."

I was still wondering where she was going with this line of questioning. She was interrogating me like a witness of Perry Mason.

"OCD is not just a symptom of university life, Steve. I think you know that. If you don't keep working on yourself, your obsessions might change, but you will always have some form of this disorder."

She had to spoil things, I thought, *like rain on a parade.*

"Maybe you're wrong. I'm doing better, Susan."

"You're just more at ease right now."

"I'm also more determined to change my life."

"Please explain, Steve."

"I want to meet girls again and get laid."

I knew the moment I said that that she would be upset. I could have phrased it better but maybe she would appreciate my honesty.

She laughed, "Isn't that normal for someone in your age range?"

"I think it's very normal and since I gave up alcohol, I haven't even talked to many girls."

"You know Steve, you did a great job giving up the booze. I know it couldn't have been easy but you really persevered."

"I was terrified, Susan."

"I know you were, so I must ask what are you scared of now?"

I wasn't quite sure again what she wanted me to say and how deep this conversation would go. A part of me wanted to walk out the door and just try to get my rocks off somewhere.

"The same thing I've always been terrorized by; not being normal."

"So, interacting with the opposite sex would make you normal."

"Well, it would go a long way but that is why I'm here."

She looked like she was going to say something cynical so I quickly continued.

"I forgot what it's like to talk to females while I'm sober."

The last statement which was true made me kind of sad as if I was the animal my brothers thought I was.

"Steve, are you telling me that you have not talked to any girls on campus in the last year or so?"

"I have been very sick and…" I wasn't sure how to answer her as I did not see her on a weekly basis but only called her when I needed help. I had not been giving her updates on my love life or lack of it.

"And what, Steve?"

"I have been too sick and too tired fighting this disease to flirt with girls. So yes, I have talked with them on occasion but I forgot what it's like to flirt with them." I was slightly embarrassed having this conversation with her but also intrigued as to what she might say as a female.

"Steve, you have to ask yourself a larger question," she said as she stared more intently at me. She was not laughing and the conversation had turned very serious and deep which frightened me. "Are you looking to get laid or have a meaningful relationship with someone?" she asked.

"I want to do whatever normal guys my age are doing."

"There is no normal. People your age behave in different ways but I'm asking you to consider whether you just want to go back to who you were."

"I'm not a drunk bastard anymore and I don't want to hurt anyone."

"I think you have answered your question, Steve."

I was puzzled. No, I did not want to hurt anyone but I figured if I was sober, it wouldn't lead to that.

"So, doc, you're saying if I just have sex with these girls then I'm no better than the drunk asshole I used to be?"

"No, Steve. I'm just asking you to put the women's feelings at the forefront of everything. If they want to have sex or whatever, that is fine. But I caution you to not just act because it fits your idea of normalcy."

"I just want to have sex already, Susan."

"That truly is sad because you have been through a lot and I was optimistic that you would be interested in something more profound."

I was starting to feel a little dizzy with the way the conversation was going. How dare she hold me to a higher moral standard just because I had suffered? She had just an inkling of an idea, perhaps a glimpse, of the wars I had been battling.

"I think it's highly unfair, Susan, that you think just because I have suffered that I should act in such an ethical manner."

"Don't forget, Steve, that it was you, some time ago, who was morally questioning your every interaction with the opposite sex."

"But, I'm not the same person!" I shouted back.

"You're wrong, Steve. You still have OCD and just because you are finishing college and entering your idea of the real world, does not mean your problems will just vanish."

I could feel my chest racing and my fists clenching. My temper was starting to flare up. I knew my suffering would never completely cease but I did believe that a lot of my problems were symptomatic of college life. Was I being naive?

I stood up, "I'm going to leave because you don't believe in me and I realize things will always be difficult for me in some areas, but college is over."

"But your life is just beginning and you need help. I would like you to start seeing me more often after graduation."

"I don't know where I will be living, but I don't think I am going to require that strong care."

"OCD is not leaving you, Steve. It doesn't just pick up and walk away."

I was standing still, but feeling very lost because I always counted on her and it looked like she did not believe in me.

"You don't believe in me, do you?" I calmly asked.

"Steve," she pleaded as I began to walk toward the door, "I never doubted you. It's the disease I doubt."

Summer 1995

That summer will always hold special memories for me. I was working at a retail store stocking shelves right after graduation. My parents wanted me to come home but I feared the loneliness that I always found myself surrounded by growing up there. So I decided to stay at the fraternity house over the summer.

It was odd, being that most of the brothers and I were not close anymore. However, since it was summer, there were just a few other people living there and John was able to arrange a sublet for me by vouching that I was changing for the better.

John was always looking out for me and it was difficult to say goodbye to him. But I knew that though he lived a few hours away from the university, we would see each other again.

"I love you," he told me again the day of commencement as he was getting ready to leave for home with his parents.

"One day, maybe I will say those same words to you," I said quietly so his parents who were looking onward wouldn't hear.

"This isn't goodbye, Steve, it's see-you-later."

I couldn't help but smile. I sincerely believed we would see each other again. I left John and then had to deal with my parents who were waiting for me at a nearby restaurant to celebrate. I had introduced them to John and they were glad that I had such a supportive friend. I was disappointed that my brothers did not come down for graduation. I was told they had other plans.

When I arrived at the restaurant, my parents pleaded with me to come home. Well, at least my father did.

"What are you going to do here, Steve?" he shouted across the table so everyone else in the restaurant could hear.

"I don't know, Dad, but I will be back in the fall. I promise," I didn't know where I would be in two months as I knew I had to get out of this college town at some point and get on with my life. However, I was terribly frightened of living an isolated life in an isolated town in New York.

"What are two more months going to do?"

"It will give me time to think about what I want to do for the rest of my life."

"You can think about things back at home, Steve."

My mom then chimed in, "If he wants to stay, let him."

I knew my mother may have meant well but it almost came across as if she didn't want to keep dealing with me.

"What do you want to do for a living?" my dad asked more compassionately.

"I'm not sure, but I want to get a temporary job here just to make some money and see if it's anything I want to pursue."

"What kind of work?" my dad continued. He was coming across as compassionate but persistent.

"Maybe something in retail."

"Unless you are a manager, you are not going to make much."

"Well, I'll start at the bottom and maybe pursue management if it's a fit."

"Here or back home?"

"Here, Dad. Then if I like it, I can pursue something in retail at a higher level back home." I realized I had raised my voice out of frustration but it seemed as if my dad was reaching his breaking point.

"Son, I know you can do a lot of things and if you want to pursue management at a retail store, I believe back home would be the best option."

"Dad, can't you just give me a few months?" I snapped back.

"Stevie," he said calmly and then paused. He was shaking his head.

"What, Dad?"

"I only want what is best for you and we love you. We would give our lives for you so of course, I can give you a few months."

I felt good again. It reminded me of all those times growing up when I was able to confide in my father and he would help me get through everything. Then again, who was I kidding? He had always been there for me, even while I was away. He was a great man and I wanted to be as successful in life as he was. I was just unsure as to what would develop for me in life.

About a week later, I applied to a giant toy store and was hired on the spot. When I told my father, he was happy because he said if things go well for me there, I can always transfer to another location closer to home. It was sad and beautiful listening to my father. Beautiful, because he wanted to be close to me and watch me succeed. Sad, however, because I was not as interested in the job as I was in other activities.

On my first day there, I literally met the most beautiful woman I had ever laid eyes on. We made eye contact a few times and it seemed as if she was smiling at me. I knew I would have to make the first move, so I took one last glance at her before acting upon my impulse to ask her out. She had an athletic-looking body, long blonde hair, and a sexy face complete with freckles and dimples. I knew this would be the perfect test to see if I still had any fuel left in the old tank.

"I usually don't do this."

"Do what?" she replied.

"I almost never approach a girl who I know is with someone."

"What makes you think that I'm involved with someone?"

She was giggling and I could tell she was enjoying the conversation.

"Please tell me I'm wrong," I pleaded.

"I'm not going to say that either."

"What in God's world are you trying to say to me?" I asked again.

"I'm not trying to say anything. I'm just trying to find out who you are and what your story is," she delicately stated.

"Do you want to know my name?" I asked.

"How did you know I was with another man?"

"You're just so damn beautiful."

"Thank you, that's very sweet and under different circumstances, I might keep flirting with you but I do have a boyfriend back at college."

"He's a lucky son of a bitch."

"So are you ever going to tell me?" she asked.

"Tell you what?"

"Your name."

"I'm Steve and I think I'm falling fast for you."

"You don't believe in love at first sight, do you, Steve?"

"I'm not sure of anything right now. In fact, I feel a little bit dizzy."

"Why don't you take a deep breath and ask me my name?"

She was still smiling but I was disappointed she was with someone. However, I wouldn't let that deter me.

I paused a few seconds, breathed, and then asked, "What should I call you?"

"You can call me Claire."

"What school are you in?" I asked.

"I'm entering my final year at State."

"I bet you do very well there."

"Thank you, you know you are very sweet. Are you in school, Steve?"

"I just graduated and am moving back home when September comes. But what made you choose State?"

"I'm on a basketball scholarship."

"Well, you do look very athletic, Claire."

"Thanks, sweetie, you look pretty fit too."

I went home that night and couldn't stop thinking about Claire. All I wanted to do was kiss her, just once. There was no way anything more could come of it. We were going to different places in life, but to me, that didn't matter. It would be incredible to kiss her mouth.

After a week or two, I noticed a big gorgeous rock on her finger.

"That's a very nice ring."

"It's an engagement ring."

"When are you getting married?"

"Well, not for a few years because I'm going to medical school. He's just going to have to wait."

"He doesn't want to wait?" I asked.

"Not exactly," she replied.

I noticed an opening. There was no marriage date set and it appeared as if there was some friction between the two.

"Where is he?"

"Ken lives near campus. He is waiting for me to come back for the fall semester. Why doesn't an attractive guy such as yourself have a girlfriend?"

I laughed, "I'm not boyfriend material."

"Says who?"

"I can't explain it right now."

The next week, Claire and I flirted nonstop. I would dance around the issue of the two of us possibly going out one night. However, being in unchartered waters, I needed a consultation with John, who was home. I called and told him everything. He taught me a very important lesson.

"Guys don't need a reason to have sex, but girls do," he said.

The next day at lunch, Claire was wearing a sexy skirt, and I told her how hot it was getting me.

She responded in a sly and flirtatious voice, saying, "Maybe we should take care of that tonight."

Claire showed up at my house and I was amazed at how beautiful she looked. She was wearing a short skirt and one of those tops with her belly showing. We went to a local bar. I steered the conversation toward what I was looking for, which was sex.

"I think we would have made love already, Claire, if it wasn't for your engagement," I said.

"That's a pretty presumptuous statement. However, you're probably right, but I wouldn't want to be another notch in your belt."

"You never would be."

"How am I to know?"

"Because I am still a virgin."

"I'm surprised."

"Why?"

"You don't realize how charming you are, Steve, I think you're incredible."

"Why don't we go back to my place, Claire?"

"Aren't you eager?"

"For you, yes. Very much so."

We walked to her car. I tried to kiss her, but she put her hand out to stop me.

"You know you want to."

"I do, but I'm also scared."

I leaned in to kiss her. Her mouth met mine. We got back to my place and we continued kissing each other all over. I loved the way she smelled. Kissing her neck was like a taste of heaven. Everything made sense with her and didn't feel complicated emotionally or physically like it did with other girls I pursued. I was stone-cold sober and knew she wanted me to be with her, so I entered unchartered territory and made great, passionate love to her that night. There was no question she loved it as well.

An hour later, she said her parents were expecting her home. I assumed it was going to be a one-night stand, but the next night she called and asked if I wanted to go clubbing with her.

That evening, my mind was playing tricks on me. I saw her talking with a lot of different men and I thought I heard her say that she really did not like me. I pulled her out to the parking lot to confront her.

"What's wrong?" she asked.

"It doesn't matter," I was feeling insecure.

"It does to me."

"Why do you care? You don't need my complications. You have an easy relationship back at State."

"Maybe I don't want an easy relationship. So why don't you just shoot straight with me?"

"Fine. First off, were you telling some of those guys that I was a loser?"

"Of course not. Why would you even think that?"

"Well, sometimes I hear or see things," I said. "I have obsessive-compulsive disorder. It can be very difficult to have a relationship with me. So I must ask you again: Were you talking negatively about me?"

"I would never do that."

We hugged; it just felt so right in her arms.

"You don't want to go back in there, do you?" I said.

"Of course not, I want to be with you."

We went back to my house. A few hours later when we were curled up in bed, I said: "Claire, I love you."

"I love you too. Immensely."

"Will you break off the engagement?"

"Of course. When I get back to State, I will return the ring."

"You know that I would move there if you asked me."

"I know, but you belong back in New York for at least a little while to see your family."

The next few nights, we continued to make love at my house. The only thing that worried me was that she had no phone number yet because she was moving into a new apartment. She promised that she would call as soon as she moved into her new place.

Fall 1995

I took the bus back to New York and waited three days without hearing from Claire. I was scared, so I called Claire's home.

I hesitantly dialed the phone and nervously waited for someone to answer.

"Mrs. Ramsey?" I frighteningly asked.

"Who is this?"

"It's Steve, from New York."

There was a disturbing silence for a second which felt like hours.

"What do you want?" she replied.

"It's Steve, Claire's friend."

"I know all about who you are but why are you calling me?"

"I was hoping you could give me Claire's phone number."

"I can't do that."

"Why not?"

"I can't do that."

"Why not?"

"Steve, it's over."

"What's over?"

"You and my daughter, and don't pretend like you don't know what I am talking about."

"But, I love Claire."

"Do you love Jesus Christ?"

"I'm not following."

"Why do you want to hear from my daughter?"

"I can't live without her. She is my everything."

"Can you live without Christ?"

"I can't live without Claire. That is all I know."

"Then you admit you don't know everything."

"I don't understand what you are saying, Mrs. Ramsey."

"You know exactly what I am saying."

"I'm sorry, but I don't."

"I'm terribly, terribly sorry."

"About what?"

"That Steve, you have no spirituality, religion, or even a hint of faith in God."

"How do you know this?"

"Because you don't know what you want."

"I know I want Claire. She is my everything."

"There is so much more to life than our interactions with other people."

"Mrs. Ramsey, I am begging you. Can you please give me the phone number to Claire's apartment?"

"Steve, I think the larger question is can you become a child of God?"

My parents pleaded with me to stay, but it was useless. I arrived at State that evening and checked into a hotel. At about 10 pm, I stepped out, determined to find her. Claire. I went to many bars, but couldn't locate her. I had a few beers and went back to the hotel in the wee hours of the morning. I stayed a few more nights just drinking but to no avail. Finally, when my hotel bill was getting steep, I went to a pizza shop in the afternoon. To my surprise, I saw Claire eating with a tall blonde male.

"Hi Claire," I said.

"Steve, what are you doing here?"

"I came to see you. Your mom wouldn't give me your info." I noticed that she was wearing her shiny ring.

"This is the guy you went out with?" Ken said.

"Yes," she whispered.

"I think you should leave," he stated angrily.

"Ken," she said, "go across the street. Give me five minutes with Steve."

Ken left, and I sat down.

"Why did you do this to me, Claire? Couldn't we have done this in a better way?"

"When I told my father about our affair, he claimed I was immature and should honor my commitments. Plus, to be honest, we hardly know each other."

"Since you left me, I've been in agony." I started to cry, "I love you."

"I don't know if I can say the same thing," she said.

"So you just used me so you wouldn't have to be alone?" Tears were running down my face and my head finally collapsed on the table. "Please don't leave me. I have nowhere to go."

"I should have handled the situation better, but I'm sorry. It's over."

"But nobody gets me like you do, Claire. I have no one and nothing back in New York."

"You have your parents and you should feel blessed each day that you have such dedicated people in your life."

"I don't see it exactly that way."

"I know but that's exactly why you must go on and find yourself, Steve. I can't give you what you want or better yet, need."

We hugged and she walked out. My life was over. I got on the next flight and came home.

The next few days I spent in bed, watching television. All of my college friends lived far away and my brothers were away as well. I cried a couple of times a day. I would have married Claire and moved anywhere in the country to be together. I couldn't believe it was over.

My parents would call me to the table for dinner and try to make conversation, but I only wanted to lie in bed. I would watch movies until 3 am and finally fall into one of my peaceful dreams. They would always be of Claire. I would dream of caressing and kissing her body. When I awoke in the afternoon, I would be more depressed knowing it wasn't real. It was all so futile. I didn't even know her phone number and she certainly wasn't going to call me.

The weeks and months dragged on, and my obsessive-compulsive symptoms were growing worse. During dinner, I kept thinking my parents were talking about Claire.

One night, my dad asked, "Are you planning on looking for a job soon?"

"Did you mention Claire?" I asked in confusion.

"No. What in God's name are you speaking about?"

"I think you and Mom are talking about Claire when I hear you speak."

My mom was stunned. "You need help Steve," she said.

"I know. And there are other problems, too."

"What?" my mom asked.

"It's common among OCD sufferers, but when I'm driving, I keep thinking I'm running over people, so I have to go back over the same road multiple times. That's why I don't even like going to the convenience store."

My mom started crying and my dad followed her into their bedroom to console her.

While they were speaking, I still thought they were talking about all the horrible things I did to Claire.

"I didn't rape her!" I cried out loudly.

My parents opened the room and both looked puzzled. My dad said, "Stevie, did you say what I think you said?"

"Probably."

"Steve…" he continued to say more but I got choked up and walked away to my bedroom to cry on my pillow.

My mind was wandering rapidly back and forth as my tears wet the pillow. Was I a rapist? Was I that horrible person that for the last few years I tried to avoid becoming?

The next afternoon, my dad approached me. "Steve, I want you to return back to your social worker. You obviously have a good rapport with her and Mom will drive you there."

"Can you go with me?" I pleaded.

"Stevie, don't hide from your mother. She loves you and wants the best for you. Plus, you know I work every day."

"Dad, can I ask you a question?"

"You know the answer."

"Well, do you think you would be happy without Mom in your life?"

"I think I know where this is leading. I knew your mom before we decided to spend the rest of our life together a lot longer than your current female friend."

It sounded somewhat derogatory as if it was something my mom would say so I just stopped the questioning and left the room.

The next day, I talked with Susan as my mom read a magazine in the waiting room.

"What happened this summer, Steve?" she said.

"Talking about it isn't going to help."

"Why don't you give it a try? You've never had a problem conversing with me. Why now?"

"Everything's changed," I really meant it this time. I spent so much time gearing up for sex and now my life was plummeting just as she had predicted.

I told her very little about Claire because I did not want her to know how correct she was about my rituals and my obsessive-compulsive disorder.

"Do you have any social interactions at all?"

"Not besides the twisted conversations I have with my parents," I replied. I was lost trying to piece together how my life had gone from being just so insane to depressing and insane.

"You were right. I was wrong. My OCD did not just walk away. It just changed symptoms."

"So, Steve do you understand now why I was so concerned when you came to me a few months ago about seeking out sex?"

"Yes, but I also love Claire."

"Do you think she loves you?"

"I think she can if I get better."

"Why, Steve, don't you think about the people who do love you?"

"I don't know any."

"Get your head out of the sand. You have two," she seemed like she was getting upset at our back-and-forth discussion and wanted me to focus. That was not possible as I couldn't see the forest for the trees.

"Who?"

"Your parents love you very much."

"I don't want to go there, Susan. What about all my OCD symptoms?"

"Well, the disorder is permanent. In other words, there is no cure as you know, and as has been told to you by myself and others."

"So, what are we going to do?"

"Well, I've got to wrap things up now but next week, I really need to hear more about your symptoms and more about your relationship with Claire."

"What difference does it make?"

"I'm hoping to manage the disease like a doctor would for cancer or diabetes. However, the more depressed you become, the more fierce the symptoms will become."

"Why do I have it?"

"Nobody really knows definitively the cause of it," she said, "but there appears to be a genetic link."

The next week, I talked with her again as my mom read a magazine in the waiting room as if she had no care in the world. She either didn't care or didn't know how to show it.

"What happened this summer, Steve?"

"Talking about it is not going to help."

"Steve, what happened this summer?"

"I don't want to talk about it."

"Then, why are you here?"

"Because my mom brought me."

"Do you do everything your mother asks?"

"I don't know."

"So, back to the original question: Steve, what happened this summer?"

"Why is it so important for you to know?"

"I want to help you."

"You can't help me. I'm beyond help," I sincerely believed this and was seeing her just to placate my parents, primarily my dad.

"We can dance around in circles for this entire session but why don't you just tell me what happened?"

"I fell in love, okay."

"Go on."

I assumed she really wanted to know so I decided to open up.

"I met the most beautiful, passionate woman in the world and I lost her. I gave my virginity to her as well, but the bottom line is that I lost her. She doesn't want to have anything to do with me anymore. This is difficult for me because I love her and I need her more than anyone I've ever needed in my life. I thought my life was bad before I met her, but then after meeting her and getting to know her, I now am aware that my life was as empty as could be. I feel nothing without her and a general lack of purpose without having her by my side. The pathetic, irritating, and most offensive thing to me is that she not only doesn't want to have anything to do with me, but I'm the one, yes, I'm the one who drove her away. I believe I may have taken advantage of this wonderful girl. I sense I may have made a colossal mistake by imposing my will as well as my strength to make her submit to my physical demands. I'm no good and I am certainly nothing but trouble. I just don't know the truth because she won't return my messages and maybe it's because deep, deep, down, we both know how evil I really am."

"Steve, are you implying that you raped her?"

"I hope not but I fear I did."

"When? When, Steve?"

"Are you going to talk to the police?"

"No."

"Are you going to tell Claire that I raped her?"

I couldn't avoid interrogating her as I did with my parents, every night. I kept my head down to avoid eye contact, out of shame.

"Steve, please listen to me. You had intercourse with her numerous times so when did you rape her?"

"I don't think I did, but I need certainty."

"That's the problem. The problem is that you're doubting yourself."

That night, I asked my parents if OCD ran in the family. My dad explained that he had a small case, but it's manageable and nowhere near as bad as mine.

"I struggled with it a little as a boy with washing my hands but it is nowhere near as intense as it is with you." I wasn't sure if I believed him and I was quite sure he was hiding things from me, fearful that I would make the same mistakes he did as a young man.

February 1996

I picked up the ringing phone. The most pleasant voice was on the other end.

"Steve?" the voice said.

"Is this Claire?"

"Yes. How are you?"

"Hanging in. Why are you calling?"

"I miss you."

"Well, I'm suffering every day without you."

"Steve, do you want to see me?"

"You know I do, but what about Ken?"

"Things are not going well between us."

"I'll be there Friday evening."

I told my parents. Though they were upset, I knew they couldn't stop me from going.

I arrived at Claire's. When she opened the door, it was like God had breathed new life into me. I gave her a bouquet of roses. She embraced me. She had cooked dinner for me, and we both sat down. We both had beers, but I could barely eat while I kept my eyes on her.

"Why do you keep staring at me?"

"I just never thought this day would come, but where's Ken?"

"He's at his apartment; I told him I wanted to be alone for the weekend."

"He would probably kill me if he found me here, wouldn't he?"

"Probably, does that make you nervous?"

"No. Because I would go through an immense amount of torture to be with you."

"Why?"

"Because you're the most beautiful female that I have ever laid my eyes on," I said.

"I think you're beautiful, too."

"You know if we went to high school together, I would never have spoken to you."

"Why not?"

"I would have been scared to approach you; I didn't have any confidence back then."

"Well, Steve. You seemed confident this summer. And though a little nervous, you seem to be brimming with confidence tonight."

"Does that turn you on?" I asked.

"Very much so."

I led her to her bed. When I kissed her neck, the scent of her brought me back to those hot summer nights. As we made love, I knew my doubts were terribly ridiculous as she wanted me intensely.

As we cuddled, an hour later, she asked, "How's your OCD going?"

"I'm trying my hardest, but it's been rough."

When I awoke the next morning, I was feeling stressed and agitated. I had thoughts that I wasn't making love with Claire, but that I had raped her. This was common with me. During the sex, I felt exhilarated. But afterward, my disease would creep back into my mind. I knew I was losing it. Did I rape her this summer? If I did, why would she have invited me here?

"Claire, did I rape you at any time in our relationship?"

She looked disappointed and said, "Don't ask stupid questions."

"I can't help it."

"So you want me to engage in your warped disorder?"

"No, I just want the truth."

"I don't like talking about what we do when we are alone. But no, you haven't raped me."

"You sure?"

"I'm sure."

"So yes or no?" I screamed. "Did I rape you?"

"No!" she yelled back. "And I don't want to talk about it any further."

"I'm sorry."

"Why are you acting this way?" she said.

"Because I have a severe case of OCD. It's acting up, and there is nothing I can do to stop it."

"Do you have any medication on you?" she asked.

"Yes, but it's not helping," I said.

Claire turned sweet again. She wrapped her arms around me.

"I'm sorry I got ticked off. I know it isn't your fault, but I find it frustrating to deal with."

"Everybody does," I said flatly.

"What do you mean by that?" she asked.

"I just know that it's tough to have a relationship with someone whose perceptions of reality are off."

"I'm doing the best I can, Steve."

"I bet you have an easier relationship with Ken."

"I told you this summer that I wasn't looking for something easy."

"It's easier to say it than to really mean it."

"Whatever happens, it won't affect my choices."

"Did I rape you?"

"I'm not answering you,"

"Did I rape you?" I screamed.

"I can't handle this, Steve. Sometimes you are so charming and captivating, and other times you drive me up a wall. Reluctantly, I have to ask you to leave, Steve."

"What?"

"I'm sorry. But this isn't going to work."

"I thought you loved me."

"Steve," Claire said, "you need help and I can't give it to you. Plus, I'm going to marry Ken."

"Why did you invite me here?" I was sobbing frantically but it didn't seem as if she cared anymore about me or my affliction. She was suddenly being so cut and dry, just asking me to leave like I was an intruder. Maybe all women, from my mother to her, were like that. They cared about their own self-preservation rather than trying to help the people closest to them. I was so desperate for her reassurance but she continued.

"I was angry with Ken and wanted to see if our relationship could go anywhere, but I was clearly wrong."

"So you used me again."

"It's not like you didn't enjoy yourself."

"Just take me to the airport. I'm not even going to ask for your number. You have mine. I don't think I have to tell you this again, but Claire: I'm madly in love with you."

I was crying again and she hugged me.

"I hope you find someone worthy of you," she whispered in my ear.

It occurred to me on the way home that maybe Claire wasn't who I thought she was. Yes, she was beautiful and compassionate, but she had exhibited a total lack of regard for my feelings. But deep down, I knew it was me, the loser, that had driven this wonderful woman away just as I had driven everyone who cared about me away.

I thought over the next several months about contacting John but I never did. He had called my house several times but I always told my parents to tell him that I would call him back. However, all the time, I knew that there would be no response from me. My life was awful and I would just drag John down with my ship just as I had done with Claire. I knew it was not a see-you-later with John, but a final goodbye as he would not continue to call me forever.

July 1996

"When are you going to get a job?" my dad demanded.

"I don't know," I said. "And I don't drive, so where could I work?"

"Anywhere," he said. "I don't care how much you make, just as long as you do something."

"Dad, I did not graduate with honors so I can work at some low-level job."

"Well, it is better than doing nothing, which is all you are accomplishing now."

My dad refused to see that the skin of my hands was wearing away due to my excessive washing. The guilt of my increasingly bad thoughts was getting to me. The more I thought about them, the more I washed. Dad meant well, but he was growing frustrated with me as well. Perhaps my mother was talking with him about how I was on a road to nowhere and that they shouldn't invest much more time in me. They had better children with more things going for them. I was reminded of something a doctor told me a while back about how I think too much and how dangerous thinking, rather than living, could be. Perhaps she was right, but I was a thinker. Quite an obsessive one, at that.

A few weeks later, I got a job as a bank teller. I was able to walk to the place. The work was difficult, but I was glad to be doing something productive. However, three months later, my supervisor called me into his office.

"Steve, we are letting you go," he said. "You just didn't live up to expectations."

"How so?" I said.

"Well, frankly," he said, "you are not quick enough to be a teller."

"I think I have been pretty efficient," I said.

"I'm not saying you haven't done good work here," he said. "I just don't think that this is the right place for you. You should gather your stuff and leave."

I knew my boss was correct. I was always checking things, so I couldn't get any meaningful work accomplished. I always had to review my work time after time so it took me longer to complete a task, just as it did with my studies in college.

I went home and told my dad what transpired at the bank.

"I'm proud of you for trying," my dad said.

The next few days, I stayed in bed and watched TV. Homecoming was coming up, but there was no way I would let any of my friends see what had become of me.

The only good thing the job did for me was to distract me from my obsessions with Claire. Unfortunately, at my jobs, I would obsess over every detail of the work and how it could hurt people that I never got anything done. Now that I was unemployed, though, I thought about her nonstop. I wondered what she was doing.

"How are things?" Susan asked.

"I got fired from my job," I said. "So, I'm home again."

"What's that like?" she said.

"Well, I think about Claire often."

"And how does that make you feel?"

"Depressed, lonely; wondering how I can contact her?"

"What do you mean, Steve, by contact her?"

"I want to find out for sure if I raped or violated her," I said.

"She is not going to talk to you."

"How do you know Susan? Have you spoken to her?"

"Of course not."

"Are you sure you didn't just tell me that you spoke to Claire?" I asked. Again, I was avoiding eye contact out of deep shame.

I realized I was getting more desperate and sicker but I felt a general disregard toward my well-being. It reminded me of when I was a college student and could barely walk back to my room without constant checking. Then, I couldn't stop obsessing about my teachers. Now, I could only focus on my relations with Claire and nothing else.

"When did I tell you that?" she asked with a touch of irritation.

"I thought I saw your lips move."

"So you keep hearing things, Steve?" she asked.

"I guess so. So you did not speak to Claire?"

"No, I did not. Are you questioning your parents as well?"

"Yes, every night."

June 1997

I was determined to drive, so I took the car to a local shopping plaza. I knew I had hit someone, so I drove through the small parking lot about 50 times in a panic. The security guard must have noticed me because a cop car got behind me and flashed his lights. I stopped, got out of the car, and approached the young officer.

"What's going on here?" he asked.

As I struggled to show him my driver's license, he saw my worn-out hands.

"Were you in a fight? Because your hands look like they have been bleeding," he said.

"No," I said, looking at the raw skin on my fingers. "I'm just trying to get home."

"Why are you circling this lot repeatedly?" he said.

"I'm stuck, officer," I said. "I'm trying to get home, but I'm suffering from OCD, and I can't seem to get back. My parents are home and can confirm my story."

The officer seemed empathetic and followed me back to my house where he rang the doorbell. My dad greeted the officer who told him what had occurred. My father confirmed my sick condition.

"Is he under a doctor's care?" the officer asked.

"Yes, he is," my dad replied.

For the first time in my life, I saw tears from my dad's eyes.

The officer left and I was still surprised at how sad my strong father looked. This had taken a lot out of him but it was his genes that led me to this condition. I wondered if he felt any responsibility. There were many things I was curious about regarding my father and wanted answers. He never talked much about his childhood or his strained relationship with his parents. I asked him if we could go into the house and sit down for a conversation because I needed to get to the bottom of this puzzle.

"Dad, why didn't your mother love you?"

"I think she did but had a tough time expressing it. I had verbal and facial tics like you, Steve, and she was ashamed of me. She would have friends over and I embarrassed her."

"You could never embarrass me, Dad. I love you. I love you unconditionally."

I was shocked at the words that were coming out of my mouth. I always felt this way but saying them, now that was a drastic change.

"Me too, son. Steve, I've been waiting for years for you to tell me that you love me."

"Sometimes, Dad, I have trouble expressing how I feel for you but you are not alone either in your plight. So what happened when you had these tics, and where was your father?"

"Your grandfather was a good man, Steve, but he was a weak man. He couldn't stand up for me, or to my mother."

"So, do you think he loved you?"

"Why would you ask that?"

"Because if a father can't stand up for his son, can he really love him?"

"It's a good point but it's far more complicated than it appears. It was a different time."

"I think you make excuses for your dad."

"Maybe I need to."

"So you were like me, huh Dad?"

"Nobody's like you Stevie, but I had OCD back then. Just nobody knew what to call it when I was a child."

"So what did your mother do when you had tics?"

"Nothing that your precious mother would ever do. I want you to know that as impatient as she becomes with you, it's always out of love and concern, not anger or embarrassment."

"Sometimes, I think Mom is so disappointed in me, Dad."

"She loves you, don't ever forget. Friends leave…but family stays."

"Dad, will you please tell me what your mother did to you?"

"It does not matter. What matters is that you understand that Mom loves you."

"I think I get it."

"When I was a boy, I believed that if I thought of a naked woman, I would need to wash my hands. So all during puberty, I would think of Marilyn Monroe and run to wash my hands every 30 seconds. My hands were as raw as yours are."

"What's your point?"

"My mother told me I was embarrassing her when I would keep running to the bathroom while she had company. I couldn't control myself. The more I tried not to think of Marilyn Monroe, I would think of her again. And then I'd be dashing into the bathroom every minute to wash my hands again. Soon, I couldn't even leave the bathroom. I would stand in front of the sink for hours at a time, with my hands under the water. Well, one time, she had company over and my mom was getting angry over the shame she had for me. At first, she yelled out to me to go to my bedroom but I did not have the power to do that. So, after a few minutes, she went to my room, crying, and got one of my belts from my closet and you know the rest."

"Tell me, Dad."

"Why?"

"It will help you to finally get it off your chest. I want to be there for you as you always have for me."

"Son, you don't need to know anymore. You've always been there and it was my mom who was not."

"Do you miss her, Dad?"

"I just wanted her to be proud of me."

"But do you miss her?"

"Yes."

"I wish I could give her a piece of my mind. I would tell her how much hurt she caused."

"She died when you were a child but she loved you as well. My father told me she would kiss the picture of you that she owned before going to bed."

"I think that was her way of telling you she was proud, Dad."

"I think so too but then again, I loved her so much that I needed to believe that."

My father was crying profusely and so I paused for a few seconds, not sure what to do, but then I put my hand on his shoulder and kissed the big guy on his cheek. A smile rose from his face.

I wanted to try hard to quell my inner demons for my dad's sake, so instead of quitting as I did with everything else, I decided to push forward and keep driving.

A few months later, I was able to take the car out daily. Each time I did so, I would return home and write in a notebook the final mileage displayed on the odometer. The next morning, I would check to see if the odometer matched my mileage chart. This was due to my fear of sleepwalking at night, getting in the car, and running people over. At the same time, I would lock my bedroom door hundreds of times to make sure I wouldn't leave the house in the middle of the night and kill people. I was so scared of what I was really capable of doing.

September 1997

The manager called me into his office and said, "This is the hardest part of my job."

I knew then I was in trouble. I had been working as a telemarketer for a mortgage company. With all my rituals, I had not been on the phone enough to be successful.

"Anyway," he continued, "I'm giving you a week's notice."

"Thanks, but I'll leave now."

This was the fifth job that I had been terminated from. My parents this time didn't even ask why I came home early. They got the point. I took a nap and dreamed of drinking beers with my old friend, John. Those good days were long gone.

I thought when I awoke about calling him, but I knew there was no turning back for me. John would always mean a great deal to me but for all practical purposes, we were dead to each other.

February 1998

"So how are you feeling?" Susan asked me.

"I have pretty good news," I said.

"Great, what is it?" he exclaimed.

"I drive now," I said. "I don't know why or how, but the fear of hitting someone has subsided."

"That's the thing about OCD," she said. "The symptoms wax and wane. Are you still thinking people are saying things when they are clearly not?"

"Still, but not as much," I said.

"This is great news, Steve, but tell me, are you still obsessing over Claire?"

"I don't know if I'd use the word obsessing, but I think a little about her every day."

"When is this going to end?"

"I truly don't know. Maybe never. I'm in love with her. But when I'm ready, I'll find out from her if I did anything wrong."

"That is delusional thinking, Steve, but we will deal with that next time."

February 1999

"Steve, what is in your hand?" Susan asked.

"It's a little cassette tape from an old answering machine that I had last summer."

"Why have you brought it here to share with me?"

"It's very significant to me."

"Do tell."

"I found it recently and it's a message that the girl I fell in love with, Claire, left for me while we were fighting. I've been playing it over and over again."

"Is that helping you?"

"I think so."

"What does she say on the tape?"

"It's a goodbye or a Dear John voicemail message in which she confides in me her true feelings."

"What does she say, Steve?"

"That it's over but she loved me."

"She said on that cassette tape that she loved you."

"Yes."

"Is that all?"

"No, she stated that she couldn't be with me anymore but had to tell me that she loved me."

"So, I see that you're staring rather intensely at that tape, Steve. Why?"

"I've been playing the recording over and over for days on end now and it's occurred to me that maybe I should give it to you."

"Why?"

"Because I need to free myself of Claire."

"Giving the tape to me is not going to free yourself. It's your thoughts about what is said on the tape that will free yourself."

"But everything has changed now, Susan."

"How so?"

"If she loved me, then maybe the possibility exists that I'm not so bad."

"Isn't that a good thing, Steve?"

"Yes, and each time I listen to this tape, I hear someone wonderful tell me she loved me, and I think…well, I think—maybe I'm not so evil."

"Maybe you are not evil at all, Steve."

"I'm not there yet so I need you to just take this tape for a while so I can be free."

"You are far from free, Steve."

I awoke again knowing that the only friend I would see today would be my therapist. I had isolated myself to a jail cell in my own home. This was definitely not the way I thought my life would turn out.

"How are you doing, Steve?"

"Not too good, Susan; I haven't worked in years, had a date, or anything."

"What about Claire?"

"What about her?"

"Do you still obsess over her?"

"You know you always ask that and you know the answer. Yes, I think and dream about her every day. I'm not in love with her anymore, but I need to find out the truth about what happened between us."

"I'm sorry. I'm afraid I haven't been able to help, Steve."

"You know none of this talk therapy helps?"

"Then why are you seeing me?"

"Perhaps I'd be worse, far worse without you."

"What other symptoms do you have?" she asked.

"First of all, no matter what I tell you, I'm not exposing my most extreme symptoms because they're too embarrassing."

"Tell me what you can."

I was scared to tell her everything, even though we had talked for years. Even though the episodes with Claire may have seemed bizarre to her, they weren't to me. However, what I was hiding, now that seemed a bit strange to me as well.

"Well, you know I do a frequent amount of hand washing. And I am pretty concerned with HIV. I've taken two tests in the last couple of months, and they have both been negative."

"Well, if what you tell me is correct, you haven't had any physical contact since Claire. So, why do you take the tests?"

Again, she was applying logic to an illogical person.

"Many reasons. The first test could have been wrong. And since I have many cuts on my hand from my excessive hand washing, I'm nervous that I'm running into contact with people who have similar cuts. Therefore, getting HIV."

"So, you're going to get these tests every few months even though you have a fraction of a chance of getting this disease?"

I decided to change the subject as I knew my symptoms could not be alleviated.

"You know it occurred to me that you are the only friend I have. You are my only social contact."

"But what about your brothers?" she asked.

She always knew how to get right to the point when I least wasted discussing the subject.

"They live on their own with their wives and kids," I said. "I don't go to family functions anymore. My grandmother comes over every so often, but I really don't want to see anyone."

"Why?"

"I simply don't want them to see me for who I am. I don't want to answer questions from relatives about my career path. For the same reasons, I maintain no contact with my best friend from college, even though we pledged to stay in contact."

The memory of him saying see you later to me and telling me he loved me brought me back to that moment. It also brought tears to my eyes.

I wondered often what had become of John. He called my house a few times after graduation but I had instructed my parents to tell him that I was unavailable. My mind drifted back to those carefree days of freshman year when John and I first started drinking brews together. It was lovely and innocent and it had all gone downhill since then.

I wanted to call back but I was embarrassed that my life never reached his aspirations for me or for myself. I also couldn't afford to get him involved in all my rituals and compulsions. I cared about him very much and I was not going to let him get entangled in my sordid life, even if he was strong enough to handle it. The truth is that I wasn't strong enough to handle it.

He had stopped trying to reach me after a few times. I guess he got the point that I didn't want to carry on our friendship, though that was far from the truth. I also desperately needed a friend besides my doctor and parents. But, trying to appear normal to the outside world sometimes left casualties, and I'm afraid John was one of them.

I realized that if I called John and explained to him the situation I was going through, he was smart and definitely strong enough to accept it.

"Steve," she repeated twice.

"What are you thinking about?" she asked.

"My old best friend from college, John. The one I stopped communicating with."

"You mean the one you refused to contact."

"Same difference."

"No, it is not the same difference," she said firmly.

"What do you want from me, Susan? OCD has casualties and my friendship with John is one of many."

"But it doesn't have to be that way, Steve."

"It does for me. I don't wish for him to see me this way."

"From what you told me previously, he cared for, if not loved you. Perhaps you can explain to him what has been going on."

"It's too late and I don't want to get him involved in my neuroses so I'm not going to call him."

"What if you wrote him a letter, Steve?"

"What would that do?"

I had to admit the idea of writing him sounded somewhat appealing. I could tell him what I wanted him to know and leave out certain details. I also wouldn't have to be confronted by him, which, knowing John as well as I do, would definitely ensue.

"I think it would be a positive first step for you in gaining some contact with the outside world, Steve."

"What can I say? You make perfect sense. I guess that's why you are the one getting paid the big bucks."

She laughed but continued, "So you will write a letter this week to John."

"Yes."

"Do you know where to send it?"

"I'm going to address it to his parents' house and I think they will get it to him if he is elsewhere."

I started to stand up and put on my jacket but she stopped me.

"There is more that could be done, Steve."

"What are you driving at?"

"Your life, to be honest, doesn't sound too good. I want to see you next week with your parents."

"Why?"

"I believe we need to get them more involved," she said.

"Fine," I said with some anger. I was concerned if I really confronted my parents, things could get ugly. I found in life that when people usually stop lying to one another and deal in reality, things can turn ugly.

A few days later, I sat down in my room with a pen and paper and wrote out the best letter to John that I could.

Dear John,

It has been what seems like forever since we spoke and even longer since I've seen you. For this, I take full responsibility. You see, I had asked my parents to lie and tell you that I was busy when you were calling my house. I also never intended on calling you back, but I miss you, brother.

I know you are strong and that you can handle the truth but I was scared to bring you down with me. You were right and I was wrong. The OCD did follow me after graduation and has taken away everything that I cherished and loved, including our friendship. I don't want to go into every detail of my hellish existence but wanted to let you know that I respect the time we spent together and that, hell, I miss you.

I also want to own up and say that I am sorry for what has happened to us. It is clearly my fault but it is only because I did not want to be real with you. I wanted you to think everything was normal, and if that meant losing you as a friend, I was willing at the time to do it.

Now, everything has changed, and I want to be genuine with you; but there are some things I can never tell you. I know that might hurt you but it hurts me more to be unable to answer your questions directly over the phone.

I took the coward's way out—for now. I need you, John. But, I just am unable to speak with you yet. I am hoping that someday in the near future we can talk and possibly get together so I'm begging you to write me back and not reject me. But again, that is all I am capable of at the moment. Please do not call me as I can't handle it yet. Just know that, well, know that I am thinking of you. Also, that I am trying hard to get better and fix things. We will speak when everything is fixed.

Love,
Steve

About a week later, a letter came for me in the mail with a Pennsylvania return address. I didn't get much mail so I was a bit surprised when my dad gave me the letter. I knew it was from John and was excited that he wrote me back but feared rejection. I was terrified that he had written a verbally abusive letter telling me exactly what he thought of me and how I disappointed him. However, deep down, I knew that was not his style and he probably had not written back so quickly if he was so upset with me. But, like always, I was letting my fears control my life and was hesitant to rip open the letter. It wasn't like I was doing anything worthwhile. I was lying in bed, feeling sorry for myself, watching movies on the Lifetime channel.

My appointment with my therapist was tomorrow so I realized that I had to open the letter now so that I could talk to her tomorrow if it was significantly unpleasant news. On that note, I tore open the letter and read something that was so honest, it left wounds.

Stevie,

Thanks for writing me. You are correct in that it has been a long time but I am sorry if you wrote me asking for forgiveness. Unfortunately, I can't offer you that. I called you numerous times to tell you that for work reasons I would be in New York, but you never returned my call. I was hoping for merely a simple acknowledgment that you appreciated my efforts but couldn't see me.

You never thought to think that I have problems too. You constantly are in your own head thinking that you have it the worst in life. My issues might not be as burdensome to me as your illness, and for that, I am deeply sorry. Though I knew you could not run away from your sickness, I never wished this on you. And, even when I became angry with you for dismissing me, I never wanted you to suffer. For your endless illness, I am sorry. However, I am angry that you thought you would bring me down, and that I wouldn't understand your pain.

You know how I always felt about you and that has not changed. To quote one of my favorite movies, "All we have left is our friendship." Yes brother, I still see you as my friend. However, I can't and won't let you dictate how this friendship goes. This will be my last letter to you and I beg you to not write me back.

Not under these circumstances, at least. I need more and you have to trust me, Steve, that you would not bring me down and that possibly I could be of value to you and even help put an end to your suffering.

So I'm afraid it comes down to this, brother. I want you to feel comfortable sharing all facets of your life with me, no matter how unpleasant at this moment it might feel. Sit with this letter a few days, longer if you need to. But know that I will not respond to any more letters. I need a phone call from you so that we can adequately discuss everything and possibly make plans to get together because as much as you want to hide your illness, I could handle it.

Also, your endless desire to be "normal," as you put it, is ridiculous. You are not normal but who amongst us is?

Now, I'm sounding like you—overly verbose and meandering.

Bottom line, Stevie: You are my brother and I love you but I will not engage in some sort of silly pen pal relationship. You need to call me so we can continue as brothers.

Love,
John
215-677-4222

P.S. It hurts me to write this as I know you like things easy but believe it or not, this whole process has been quite difficult for me as well. And though I would deny it if anyone asked, I have found myself crying at times thinking back on the times we spent together, and during the course of writing this letter.

I took a few moments to digest what I had just read. It was both blunt and affectionate. John was not willing to play my warped game of just writing back and forth as I had hoped. He was demanding more from me and I honestly did not know if I had it in me to give any more. But I did need a friend. The surprising thing to me is that he was not looking for me to call right away but to deliberate regarding this choice. And this choice could make all the difference in my recovery. I was aware that I was very sick but that if I was to ever have anything resembling a "normal" life, I needed John. For he was not just a friend but family, and more of a brother than the two I was related to.

I actually thought it was funny that he mocked me for wanting to always be normal. I chuckled out loud, envisioning one day throwing a baseball around with John, and fell back to sleep while the Lifetime channel played its meaningless movies.

The following morning, I realized that I had to discuss this letter with my therapist and that my parents were due to come today. However, in no way, shape, or form, did I want to discuss John in front of them. Therefore, when we arrived, I told them to sit outside for a few minutes while I spoke to Susan.

"I have big news regarding John," I told her.

"You wrote him, didn't you?"

"Yes, and he wrote back."

"How did that go?"

I recounted for her the details of the two letters and she responded with a typical therapeutic-like question.

"What are you going to do, Steve?"

"I don't know."

"It sounds like you are at a fork in the road and you have a big choice to make. A decision that can really affect your life and from someone whom I know you deeply care about."

"So what's the answer?" I asked.

"I'm not going to give you the answer, Steve. You know the best thing for you to do and frankly, I am tired of you always seeking the easy way out. Your mom and dad are here to see me so let's allow them in."

She sounded really frustrated with me and I was perplexed. She was the second person this week to have called me out on my bullshit. Maybe I had to stop trying to be normal and do what was best for me. I wasn't sure, though, if I was healthy enough to make those decisions and at the same time, I was not looking forward to this conversation with my parents.

When my parents walked in, Susan opened by saying, "I wanted to meet with you all because Steve's life is becoming increasingly worse, and I need to get your perspective."

"We do all we can," my dad replied as my mom sat silently.

"All the years I was growing up, Dad, you never told me you had OCD. It skipped your two favorite sons, but it got me. Never once did I get an apology from you."

"What do you want me to apologize for? I love you as much as your two brothers, maybe even more because I know how much you depend on me."

"You make me sound like a little child, Dad."

"That is not my intention."

He seemed really calm and at peace with himself. I wondered if I would ever find such inner peace but at this moment, I was growing frantic.

"Do you think I like living, Dad?" I shouted.

"That's your fault, Steve—not mine."

"Who taught you that? You're the whole reason for my disgusting existence."

My dad dropped his head in his hands and started to cry.

There was no inner peace for him either, apparently.

No progress was made on either end. I felt horrible as the one man who would give his life for me sat slumped in his chair with his head in his hands, crying. I noticed that his hair was growing grey and that there might not always be time for us to spend quality time together.

"Dad," I said as I began to cry from the realization of the toll that my life had taken from this kind soul.

"I'm sorry I've caused you pain as well. Perhaps we both share some responsibility. I'm willing to own mine if you own yours."

My dad lifted his head up and said, "I own that I could have done things differently in raising you but I just didn't know how. I did the best I could and maybe the only way I knew how."

His hands were shaking as it was evident this time and every time, how much he cared about his lonely, angry, middle child.

A few days later, I decided to call John after letting the possibilities of the phone call run through my head over and over, like a broken record. I realized that at some point, I was going to have to let someone in, besides my parents and therapist. John was different; he was a real friend that I could not only confide in but joke around with as well. However, I was still scared to call him; what if after all this time, we had nothing really significant to talk about? He knew me but maybe I didn't know him anymore. For Christ's sake, I didn't even know what he did for a living or if he had a serious girlfriend. I felt that the best thing to do would be to just call him and see if the conversation developed naturally. I didn't just want to recount my horrible tales of living with a sordid illness during the whole call. There had to be more to me than my illness—hopes, aspirations, whatever. I just lost so much time over the years consumed by my disease that I stopped thinking about what I really wanted in life since being normal was something I invented in my head. Whatever being normal was, I was not there but maybe other people who seemed so perfect on the outside weren't so normal either.

I dialed the digits that were written on the letter. I had been through this before. I had stared at the letter many times since I received it and always chose to not dial the phone. This time, I had to call because I was sick and tired of it ruminating in my head as I did with all my other thoughts.

The phone rang on the other end, and for a second, I thought maybe John would not be home and I could just leave a message. This would put the ball back in his court,

but before I could obsess anymore, I heard a familiar voice.
"Hello?"

"John, it's Steve."

"I knew you would call," a confident but friendly voice said to me.

"That's good because I didn't know what I was going to do."

"Well, you always take the easy way out of things, Stevie, but I wasn't going to let you this time."

I wasn't sure what to say exactly but it was comforting to hear a familiar voice that carried with it both confidence and comfort.

"How did you know I would call?"

"Because you're my brother."

"That means a lot to hear, especially after all these years."

"How bad have things got, Stevie?"

"Honestly, pretty horrible, but right now I want to hear about what you are doing. Any special ladies I should know about?"

"There was one but…" he paused.

"What is it, John?" He sounded a little choked up and his confident voice had deteriorated momentarily.

"There was a special woman, but we got married and divorced all within the last year."

"I'm so sorry, John. What happened?"

He went over the details of how he met this beautiful woman in a bar in Philadelphia which led to a quick romance without either of them really getting to know each other really well.

I wanted to ask a lot of questions without being pushy but he knew that.

"Ask away, brother. I know you have questions."

"I don't want to pry."

"Yes, you do," and he laughed.

I thought we would continue to speak frequently during the rest of our lifetime. We had so much in common but time and circumstances did not allow it. Sometimes, in war, a soldier loses a battle, and for me, this battle was my friendship with John. We never spoke again after that one time. However, I always kept him close to my heart because as he said that day, we were "brothers." He was a great brother, friend, and man, but I couldn't bring back the years that had slipped by us. The information from him about his marriage and eventual divorce sadly made me realize that too much time had gone by to have a friendship. I cared for him deeply but knew this was the end.

September 2000

My mother finally decided to play a more active role in my social life. Once a week, we went out for dinner. It was a lot of fun and I enjoyed spending time with her, despite her not being the warmest person on earth. The dinners also gave me a chance to do something. I would shower, shave, and try to look my best when we went out together. My grandmother would also join us often. She was widowed. This happy activity, however, would come to a sharp conclusion a few months later.

I told my mother that I was no longer going out with her or my grandmother to restaurants. It was too scary.

Somehow, I got it in my mind that I could either unconsciously or consciously be putting nails or rocks in the food. Ketchup bottles were the trickiest for me since they could be used over and over again by different customers. My mother asked once if she could take me to a supermarket. I told her "no," because there I could put rocks and dirt in the cereals, ice creams, etc. My mother had grown shocked at what had become of me. I confronted her in pain.

"Do you still love me, Mom?" I asked.

"Of course I do," she said.

"Maybe this is the best that it is going to get. Maybe I am lost and will never find myself again."

"Don't say that, Steve," she pleaded. "This can't be it."

"What if I don't ever get better? What then?"

"Then I will continue to take care of you."

"Won't you reach a point when you will want to quit taking care of me?"

"No."

"Why is God putting me through this? Why won't he reach out to me?"

"When you're ready for him, he will be ready to take care of you."

September 2002

I had started to think less often of Claire since my mind was preoccupied with so many other obsessions. However, I fell asleep one night and had a bizarre dream. I was seeing a psychiatrist, but the Dr. was Claire.

"I never wanted to see you suffer," she stated.

"Probably not true," I said. "I'm suffering immensely because of you."

"I'm not sure what you want me to do."

"I want you to alleviate my pain."

"It is not me that you seek, but someone higher," she said.

I woke up and knew what Claire meant. I believed that if I was God, I would just come forward.

I'd say, "Here I am. Love me, no questions asked."

Why wasn't he doing that for me? I wondered inside my head.

September 2003

I was just about ready to put Claire behind me when I arrived for my session with Susan.

"I feel better about knowing that I will never end up with Claire," I said.

"Great. You are making great strides, Steve. So why don't we work on your issues surrounding food."

"I want to, but I need closure."

"With Claire?"

"Of course."

"What does that entail?"

"Well, I'm going to call her at her home."

"How do you know she is there?"

"I don't, but I will talk to her mother."

"What are you hoping to accomplish?"

"Just to be able to put this chapter to rest."

"It's been eight years. Do you really think her mother will help you get in touch with her?"

"I really don't care," I was starting to feel the tears drop from my eyes. She offered me a tissue but I refused. "But I'm not going to be a victim anymore."

October 2003

"Hi, Mrs. Ramsey?" I asked.

"Yes. This is she."

"Can I speak to Claire?"

"Claire doesn't live here. Who may I ask is calling?"

"Steve," I said, while I trembled with fright.

"Steve who?" she questioned.

"Steve from New York."

"I remember you. What do you want?"

"Just to know how Claire's doing."

"She's fine. Very happy."

"Can you put me in touch with her?" I said.

"I'm sorry. She's married with kids. I can't do that."

"Will you tell her I called?"

"I'm afraid I can't do that either. You have done enough harm, Steve."

"But I have no one to speak to," I started to cry. "Things have gone bad for me and I need her."

"You don't need her, Steve. You will always have someone to turn to."

"Who?" I needed to know the answer to my problems.

"Jesus Christ forgives and accepts all who come to him," she stated.

"But I'm a Jew."

"So was Jesus."

"I can't."

"Then you will continue to suffer," she said.

November 2003

I walked into Susan's office and related the details of the phone call.

"How do you feel?" she said.

"Just stop it," I said.

"Stop what?"

"Quit asking me how I am. Clearly, I'm not well. Talking endlessly about my condition isn't helping anyone."

"What do you want?"

"I want a new life. I want to stop the insanity, the compulsions, the irrational thinking."

Tears were running down my face.

"What could I do? I've done everything I know how to help you," she pleaded.

"Do something different but please, don't make me come here, tear out my damn soul, and empty all this dirt on the table, thinking it will lead to an improvement. I'm not coming to talk anymore."

"I realize you're angry but I can't have you come here, throw a temper tantrum, and dictate the terms of our therapeutic relationship."

"Then, go to hell."

I went home and never saw Susan again.

It was another failed relationship but I had grown accustomed to such connections ending, and with time, I knew I could put this into perspective as well.

December 2003

I woke up a little anxious and reached for the telephone. I wanted to call Claire's mother just so I could feel closer to her. I called during daytime hours because I figured nobody would be at home. Mrs. Ramsey was the only woman who offered me a plan. I listened to her voice mail as I had on other days, and quickly hung up without leaving a message.

January 2004

I woke up and remembered what I had been dreaming of the night before. It involved a female from college, but not Claire. It was no one I could put a name to. I was in dire need of companionship. I dialed the first three digits of Mrs. Ramsey's phone number, paused, and hung up without completing the call. I needed to work on my other issues, but maybe I was starting to win the fight by not following through with the call.

February 2004

Grandma.

I loved my grandmother very much. However, I received word from my mother that she was in the hospital dying. She was in her early 80s. I didn't need to ask what was making her sick. She always told me that she wanted to join my grandfather again and that she said that she would see him when she passed. I found it strange that a member of my family held such a religious or spiritual connection to the world around her. I was spiritually lost, but she was so firm in her belief in an afterlife, and what God had in store for her. She was such a sweet woman. I remembered back to when our family moved to our house in New York. I was only four years old. My parents were busy packing and she and my grandfather, whom she affectionately called "babe," took me to Friendly's. I was so excited to be going out since we hardly went to restaurants. My grandmother insisted that we order large chocolate ice cream sundaes, and she kept smiling the whole time. She loved me deeply. I wanted to share with her my true feelings before she left for good.

I asked my mother, "Does she know I'm sick?"

"Obviously she knows something," she said.

"How?"

"I had to tell my mother something, Steve. She's a strong woman who has been through a lot in her life. She adores you. I think you're her favorite grandson."

"I didn't know she was still interested in my life anymore."

"Why? Is it because you choose not to see her?"

"I never made that choice, I can't help the fact that I can't be around people anymore."

"Don't make me cry, Steve. I promised my mother I wouldn't. She wants to be with my father. God let her."

"How many more days does she have?"

"Maybe three, or four days tops," she said. "Now you go over to the hospital and see her."

"I can't do that, Mom," I said.

"I will go with you," she said, "so you have nothing to fear."

"You don't understand," I said, "I'm not going. If the devil makes me utter something to these sick people, people all over the place are going to die."

"What are you going to say?" she said.

"Something evil, like telling the people: 'die.'"

"Just saying the word 'Die' to someone isn't going to make them drop dead."

"Maybe a healthy person wouldn't drop dead, but for a sick person, it can cause death."

"I'm not going to debate this with you, Steve. You're so damn sick! Just go watch television."

I watched TV for the rest of the week, debating whether to go to the hospital or not. I knew, however, that my decision had been made.

Yesterday morning, my mom let me know that my grandmother had passed away. My memory drifted back to when I was only 16 years old and my grandmother was teaching me to drive in a somewhat empty parking lot of a commercial building.

"Don't brake so hard."

"I'm trying, Grandma, but it just seems so difficult."

"Try again."

"I want to quit."

"You want to quit everything. You remind me of your mother in that way."

"How so?"

"When I tried to teach her Hebrew, let alone drive a car, she was as scared as a little poodle in a room full of pit bulls."

"So what happened, Mema?"

"I explained to Mommy that without patience and composure, she would never learn the wonderful language of Hebrew."

"Did it work?"

"Not at first, but I kept teaching and your mom kept learning. And what does your lovely mother do now? Well, she is a successful school teacher."

"I'm not good at anything."

"Hogwash."

"I'm not," I insisted.

"Double hogwash."

"Sorry."

"Quit your apologies and drive up to this corner and parallel park next to the red car."

"I can't do it."

"So it's your attitude that needs adjusting, not just your driving."

"Mema, I don't know what you want me to do but I can't parallel park, and I'm not too good at reading Hebrew either."

"Well, I was at your Bar Mitzvah and you did great, even if it was hard for you. As for the driving, you will learn how to parallel park if it's the last thing I teach you."

"Don't say that!"

"Well, I'm not going to be able to hold your hand forever so you better get this parking thing down pat."

I drove my car next to the red car in the somewhat desolate parking lot and tried to parallel park behind her. It was an expensive-looking car and I was scared that I might hit it so I stalled for a moment or two.

"I said I'm not going to live forever!" she shouted in my ear.

"It's a nice car and I don't want to get in trouble."

"Stop thinking so much and do it. You tend to overthink your way out of every little problem, Stevie."

To this day, I don't know if I was just tired of hearing her yap at me or I just loved her too much to let her down but I did successfully parallel park the car.

For several weeks, Grandma, or Mema as my brothers and I affectionately called her sometimes, took me out on the road every day to learn how to drive. Only, she was not merely teaching me how to drive but rather how to gain self-confidence. Now, with my Mema gone, I was scared as to who would push me to be my best self. I couldn't bear her being gone so I went into the kitchen to talk with my mother.

"I'm not going to the funeral."

"My mother would have expected more from you, Steve."

"I suppose she would, but I think she would still love me."

The day of the funeral came and I forced myself to attend. I stood in the back as her body was put to rest. I wanted to go by the casket and just tell her how much love and appreciation I had for her. I was too sick to even do that. I was scared she would hear me say something cruel even if there was no God there. My disease was killing me and destroying everything in its path. I lost my grandmother who was my own blood, and I couldn't even will myself to say goodbye. What a horrible existence! What a pathetic lonely feeling.

August 2004

My parents sent me with their hard-earned money to the best OCD clinic in the nation. It was in Ohio. Although I feared flying, my parents begged me to go. They showed me all the literature from the clinic about how they could help me. Little did they know that I was beyond help. There was no one like me in this world.

It was a beautiful home with a warm golden air that hugged it. It had a long, lush garden by a crystal blue lake that glittered dreamily in the afternoon sunlight, but the people that populated the house were weary and sick. The patients looked old even at young ages. They were battered and strung out looking. Their skin was gray and sickly. Their bodies were distorted and crippled. They were either too thin and frail or too heavy and disfigured. They had voraciously wild eyes and dirty uncared-for hair and clothes. They paced back and forth in chaotic rhythms through the garden paths and the house hallways, drinking coffee and chain-smoking cigarettes all day long. Some of them smelled like old dusty books and others showered many times a day, constantly washing their hands until their skin was bloody, broken, and raw. Some talked out loud violently to themselves. Others sat by themselves near the lake silently with lost eyes that seemed to stretch for miles and miles. When you talked to them, they couldn't hear you. They would simply stare into space and mumble nastily under their breath.

We had a group therapy session one day. It was focused on religion and scrupulosity. A patient named Dave confessed that he thought God was going to give him AIDS because he sinned by sleeping with a prostitute. Then, a younger patient, Billy, claimed that it wasn't God that caused harm, but rather the evil guy below who loved watching people suffer, Satan. The tone of the conversation caused me to panic. I felt like that young, scared college student who was terrified after watching *The Exorcist*.

That night, as I tried to fall asleep, I could feel the devil reach for me. It was as if he was creeping inside me.

Satan wanted me to bring my lips together and say: "Devil, take me."

I ran out of the room toward the phone in the hallway. It was around midnight, so I had to make sure none of the clinicians heard me.

"Mom!" I cried through the phone.

"What are you doing calling so late?" my mom yelled.

"Oh," I said, "nothing."

"You didn't call in the middle of the night for nothing," she said. "Now, what is it?"

"The devil's come for me," I said.

"What are you saying?" my mother screamed frighteningly.

"I think he's possessed me," I said in a panic.

"Calm down," my mother said. "You're not possessed. Where is all this crap coming from?"

"Someone was talking about him today. It got me thinking that if I ask the devil to possess me, then he will," I said.

"Then don't ask him," she said.

"Oh," I said, "so you believe there is a Satan? You admit it's possible that he can possess bodies and enslave you?"

"I don't admit to that," my mother said. "I don't know."

I was growing frantic.

"Mom," I said, "if due to my illness, I ask the devil to possess me, will he?"

"No," my mother said. "The devil is from a storybook. There are no devils that can possess you."

"How do you know?" I said. "Do you really know everything that exists in this world?"

"I know," my mother said, "because there is no devil. There is only God who blesses and curses. The devil does not have the power to do that."

I could hear my father grab the phone. "Now listen, Steve, and you listen good. There is no devil. Never was a devil; never will be a devil. So you could say whatever you're saying 100 times and more, but your mother and I will not listen to this anymore. And anyway, what you say doesn't matter because you're delusional. We know the truth. We are Jewish. We don't believe in that Catholic devil, demon nonsense. Now go to sleep!"

I hung up frustrated and fell asleep. The belief that there was no Lucifer who wished me tremendous suffering was comforting to me for the moment.

The next morning, I met with my psychologist, Sally, and told her of my rituals.

"Do you believe in God?" I asked.

"What difference does it matter?" she said. "If there was a God, nobody knows who he really is or what he is really like, anyway."

"It matters to me," I said, "because I need someone who cares. I need someone who can help me."

"The only thing that matters is what you believe," she said.

"But what if what I believe is not the truth?" I screamed.

"Forget that," she said. "We are getting sidetracked. I need to help you with your exposure therapy."

"How would we do that?" I said.

"Well," she said. "First, I would have you watch some dark and twisted films such as *The Exorcist*."

"But, I'm scared to watch that film," I said.

"That is exactly why I would have you watch it," she said. "To be scared."

"I don't get any of this exposure therapy!" I screamed. "Why do I want to get more scared?"

"Lower your voice," she angrily hushed. "If you panic, it will only feel worse."

"Fine, it's lowered."

"Steve," she said, "if you watch more and more of these kinds of films, you will become desensitized to the devil. In other words, after much exposure, you will be able to watch the movies without fearing the devil."

"Do you believe in God?" I asked.

"I'm not answering that question," she said. "You're practicing reassurance."

"Oh, really!" I said, with a touch of sarcasm.

"Yes," she said, "and I don't appreciate your tone."

"Screw you and the stupid idea that you can help people by forcing them to do things that they are terrified of doing," I said, and I walked out.

Later on that evening, I met with Sally again. I promised that I would never verbally abuse her.

"Steve, I want to help you. There is hope for you."

"But," I said, "you won't answer my questions."

"You know why I won't," she quickly replied.

"Do you believe that the devil could make me kill people, rape them, and poison their food?"

"Steve, you're losing touch with reality."

"I'm going to murder people because of the devil and not even remember it," I screamed in panic. "Isn't that horrible?"

"Steve," her voice grew louder and more impatient, "forget all that. Tomorrow is the group outing. I need to know if you're going."

"Why?" I said. "Isn't this important?"

"If you don't, you will be out of compliance with the rules."

"What are you saying?"

"I'm saying that the staff and I might ask you to leave."

"I'm not going anywhere, especially not outside these doors."

"Why?"

"I can destroy lives, not remember it, and keep doing it."

I didn't go on the group outing but stayed in my room the whole time.

I was dismissed the next day. My poor parents had to schlep all the way to Ohio to pick me up since I was scared to be alone. I was an adult but felt more like that scared child who waited for his dad to pull the car into the driveway to reassure him that he was okay. It was much the same feeling as I waited in the room for my parents to arrive and try to make things easier.

November 2004

For several weeks following my return home, I stayed inside. There was no outside contact for me. My life as I once knew it a long time back was over. I could hear my mom cry at night from the other room and I listened with great, overwhelming sadness.

I came to her one night when the crying was just too devastating and loud, and I begged her, "Please stop."

"I can't!" she cried. "I've lost my son. I've lost my baby."

"I'm sorry you feel that way," I said, "but I love you, Mom."

"I love you too," she said. "I pray every night to God for him to heal you. I know your grandparents are praying somewhere in heaven as well. How about tomorrow after your doctor's appointment, we all go to Wendy's?"

"I have a doctor's appointment tomorrow?" I asked.

"Yes, you can't go on like this," she said.

"So I have to leave the house," I said.

"I know you're scared," she said, "but you won't leave our side."

"You and Dad will watch that I don't do anything evil?"

"Of course, Steve."

"I can't go, Mom. I love you but I'm sorry."

"Please, Steve. I'm a fighter. Why can't you fight?"

"The stakes are too high for me, Mom."

"I want to tell you something."

"What?"

"Well, when you were in Ohio, I missed you terribly. I had to cry myself to sleep at night."

"Mom—"

"Just listen," she insisted.

I nodded my head and she continued.

"I know you find me insensitive and abrasive at times, but I've always loved you. I've been fighting this battle with you; you just haven't realized it. Let me fight with you or even for you."

"I'm not leaving the house, Mom."

"I wrote a lot when you were away. My therapist told me it would help me. I would like to show you my essays."

"I don't want to see this."

"Steve, please. I need you to read these. Maybe it will show you how much I love you."

My mom took my hand and brought me to the basement and showed me the stories about me. Stories that brought out all the feelings she masked and things I didn't even remember.

Even in the basement, I hesitated to read her words because I was scared of how much pain she had been bearing all these years.

"Mom, do I really have to read this? I know you love me. I don't want to see all that I've done to you."

"Steve, do you know who the Aztecs were?"

"Maybe I learned about them in elementary school."

"I wrote a story about the Aztecs. Please listen."

"The Aztecs were warriors who fought the enemy each day because they believed the sun fought to come out every day and therefore they must fight also. I too am a warrior. I have been called in to fight a war I didn't want to fight. I am the mother of an adult with a severe and debilitating mental illness. My son suffers from obsessive-compulsive disorder. Each day, I must fight to help him with private battles. I must help him battle the demons that have taken control of his life. These demons live only in my son's mind but they control where he lives, works, and even eats. They refuse to loosen their grip no matter how hard we fight to remove them. For a while, I was confident that we would win the battle. I would awaken each morning with a plan to beat this foe and reclaim my son's life. But the force grew even stronger and claimed more of my son's life. Still, I believed we would conquer it but I began to realize it would be more difficult than we originally thought. We tried different ways to remove this horrible demon but as hard as we worked, it continued to control my son's life. The enemy has ravished my beautiful son's life. He has grown weaker and more passive while the enemy has grown stronger and more defiant. I tell my son over and over that he must fight harder to win but he has lost his once strong spirit during the battle and has temporarily given up the fight. I have grown stronger and more determined to overcome the enemy. I am left with an image of my once strong and spirited son. I keep a picture of him on my dresser to remind me of what once he was and what he could once again be if only he would win. I have listened to my son's angry outbursts at me, his bitterness at his life, and I too have wondered why it happened to him. Yet, I have had to redirect my own bitterness before it claimed me and left me too powerless to continue the battle. Sometimes in a war, the leaders have to change their original objectives. I too have had to change my goals to less lofty ones. I am still fighting the unseen enemy but I now know the enemy will never leave my son. I am fighting for my son to control the enemy so that it no longer controls him. I am fighting so one day my son will say to me that he has reclaimed his life and no longer lets the enemy control him. Then I will be able to stop fighting."

She cried to what seemed like no end after reading her passage. I felt chills all up and down my body because I couldn't believe that my mom or anyone for that matter could love me that immensely. All this time, I never really thought I was worthy of unconditional love.

"Mom, I'm sorry I have stopped fighting."

"Just let me read you another story."

My mom was shaking terribly in her bathrobe. I was now able to see her in a whole new light. She was someone who had come a long way in her life and this was not the life she expected. I don't know who does deserve or expect such a hellish existence.

There was a long pause as my mom tried to stop crying.

"Do you remember the red London Fog jacket you bought years ago at the mall, Steve?"

"Vaguely."

"I wrote a story about it. Please, just listen."

"He gave me his red jacket and asked me to wash it for him. I looked at the red jacket there and suddenly, a flood of memories came back to me. He was a stubborn little boy of about ten. I bought him a quilted red jacket and he loved it. He was usually so fussy about everything. I would buy him things and he would like it for a day or two and then suddenly not want to wear it. But this jacket was different. He wanted to wear it all the time. One of the memories that are stored so deeply in me is the vision of the stubborn, adorable little boy walking to school carrying his books and wearing the red jacket. He liked the jacket so much that when it became too small for him, he refused to give it up. I wanted to give it to his younger brother who was the right size for it but he stubbornly refused to let it go. Of course, I gave in. He was my middle child and I had a very special feeling for him and he was my underdog and I was determined to save him. I bought my younger son a new jacket and let him have it another year. Years passed and they were not easy years for him. They were not easy years for his parents. He turned his anger on us and somehow we had to take the anger and still remember the adorable little boy in the red jacket. Years passed and he remained my special son—the one that struggled and then lashed out in anger when we tried to help. I always kept the vision of the little boy who was afraid to walk to his friend's house because of the squirrels, and the little boy who had trouble learning in front of me. They were hard years for all of us. But I stood and waited for them to get better, perhaps knowing they would always be difficult but not really wanting to believe that. Yesterday, he gave me his red jacket to wash. He bought the jacket about three weeks ago and asked me several times if I liked it. I always answered yes, because I love him with more love than I thought possible to ever feel for a child. He is a man now and not the stubborn little boy. He is a man but still a very needy man. He needs us for reassurance and acceptance and so much support. He needs us to listen to his funny stories and help him when life becomes too difficult. He needs us to love him for what he is—a very special human being who is kind and loving and bright and brimming with problems. It is because I loved him as a ten-year-old with a red quilted jacket that I am able to love him as a man with a special red jacket that needs to be washed."

When she finished, she slowly approached me and begged me to go with her to the doctor.

"Please Steve, I have suffered enough. I needed you to see that you weren't the only one who died a little each day."

"I will try, Mom. For you and for Dad, I will try to be like an Aztec."

The following day, I met with this old, slow-moving lethargic doctor. He was very kind, but I doubted he could help me or that he had any new tricks up his sleeve that would miraculously cure this disease. I proceeded to tell the psychiatrist my story with my parents by my side. At first, the doctor was unsure if he could help me since no one had been able to so far.

"I don't know," he said softly.

My mom jumped in and said, "Doctor, before you tell me that you can't help my child, I have something that I wrote last night which needs to be shared."

"Mom, please don't make me cry again," I pleaded.

"It's all right. I will listen," said the kind, gentle doctor.

"Doctor, a handsome strong man stands before me and then a sweet happy little boy so sensitive and yet so stubborn. He reaches out to me as both and though I want to pick him up and hold him as a child, I stand back and only hug him quickly as a man. I loved him through all the years and watched him put his anger on me and waited for glimpses again of that sweet golden little boy I loved so much and now when he has chosen to let me share his pain, I share it readily although tearfully for he has let me see his suffering and allowed me to touch his special sorrows, but in doing so, he has also allowed me to once again see my beautiful little boy with all of his goodness and sensitivity and it is because I once loved that little boy so much that I am able to feel his pain and take his hand and hold it through it all. I will never let it go."

She paused and then said, "Doctor, please don't let me lose my son."

"I don't want to, I want to at least try," he said. "Mrs. Goldberg, why do you think I would not be able to help your child, this man?" he asked.

My mom was shaking again as she did in her bathrobe last night. Somehow, she had the courage this morning to wake, get dressed, and try to persuade this physician to help me.

"No Doctor has been able to and you seemed reluctant," my mom explained.

"Well, I am here to tell you that I will try my hardest because I look at the three of you and there is a lot of pain here. I just can't see myself shutting the door on that and being able to look in the mirror each morning. Now Steve, before we go any further, I have already listened to you detail your affliction with great ability while your parents stayed in the room. Is that how you want to continue?"

"Yes, Doctor, I want them right by my side," I said as I clenched my mom's hand who was holding on with her other hand to my father who seemed much weaker than he was a few years ago.

"I listened to you, Steve, earlier, and I must ask—why are you scared of the phone?"

"I might dial 1-900 numbers and ring up charges," I said.

"So you are scared of losing control and doing something that will harm you and your family."

"Exactly."

"Is that why you don't leave the house?"

"Yes."

"Tell me more about that because you mentioned you used to go to restaurants with her. Why did that stop, Steve?"

"I'm scared I will put something harmful in there."

I shook as I recalled how scared I was to enter any food establishment.

"Dig deeper, Steve. I need to know."

"Well, for the same reason I don't go to supermarkets or drug stores… It's just that I'm terrified that I can get a rock or something in a package of cookies, for example."

"So again, Steve, you are terrified of losing control."

"Yes."

"What else haven't you told me, Steve?"

"Is this necessary?" my father jumped in.

"I believe I'm onto something, Mr. Goldberg."

"But Doc, he's told you almost everything," my father said, trying to protect me.

"What are you scared of, Mr. Goldberg?"

"Dad, stop. I can tell him," I said loudly.

"What, Steve?" said the doctor.

"I'm ashamed but I have involved my father in my rituals for too long. I am a bad son. I have ruined so many lives and destroyed so many relationships."

The doctor looked at me and said, "I don't believe you are bad. I just want to know what your dad does during these rituals."

"Sometimes, when I sleep and then wake up, I am 99.9% sure nothing happened. But that little .1% gnaws at me. I doubt myself and I'm scared I lost control again."

"Give me an example."

"The other morning, I awoke and thought I dreamed that I went to the ice cream parlor and put rocks in their ice cream, so I told my dad to go there and look at the ice cream bins."

"And he went?"

"He always goes. I have sent him to N.J. and Delaware and he would probably do anything I asked."

"I don't need to hear any more. This madness stops now," said the doctor.

He paused, recollected himself, and said, "You two need to stop reassuring him because it becomes an endless cycle and I suspect that is why he got tossed out of the hospital in Ohio. Am I right?"

"I take full responsibility," I said.

"This isn't about fault, Steve. I just want to see you get better but sending your father on a three-hour road trip to check something that you yourself said is highly unlikely is not working for anyone. So this is why you need your parents here today; to assure you everything is okay and that you didn't do anything that can hurt someone."

"Yes."

"Well, I will allow that temporarily if that is the only way you can get treated, but as far as the other instances, no more reassurances."

"But what if I feel anxious?"

"Then live with it. Be anxious but I think the more you deal with this anxiety, the more tolerable it will become. However, I do have to prescribe a medicine that I believe will help alleviate some of the anxiety."

As he wrote out the prescription, my parents and I got out of our seats and I asked, "Doctor, have you ever helped anyone like me?"

"It doesn't matter. Everyone's pain is different but before you leave, I just want to ask you if you have any siblings?"

"I have an older and a younger brother."

"How come you never mentioned them?"

"They're long gone. Sometimes the illness makes people leave."

"I understand."

We shook hands and I left.

It was the truth. Both of my brothers had long moved to the West Coast to get away from all the chaos I had caused. They were not terrible people. They called my parents frequently but when they visited, they preferred to do so without talking to me. They stayed at hotels and met my parents outside the home.

I used to be close to them when I was a child but all wars have their casualties and this was no different. My mom had told me that they always asked about me, and that they did indeed care, but that the pain was just intolerable. My older brother was a successful lawyer in Sacramento and the younger one was a history professor in Los Angeles. Even when I went to the clinic in Ohio, neither came by.

The same can be said of the friends I made in college, of which I had many. However, during the course of my lifetime, I had chased away many and most had just given up. There are only so many times a friend is going to invite you out to a Yankee game when you reject him each time. I would always lie and say I was busy, but actually, I was terrified of leaving the house. As a counselor at the clinic warned me, "Friends will leave."

That is why I always maintained that the only true, unconditional love is that between a parent and a child. After reading my mom's letters, I had a whole newfound love for her. She loved me so much that she was able to withstand the emotional pain of seeing me fall apart. Also, she was able to love me even when I verbally lashed out at her. It took a strong parent to do that. As for my dad, I rarely argued with him. He was a kind soul who was aging and just needed a little love and care at this point.

I needed to beat this as much for me as for my loving parents. I finally realized, after leaving the doctor's appointment, that I had now found the courage which I had been looking for all this time to fight my demons. My courage came from wanting my parents to see their favorite son rehabilitate himself.

November 2005

A year after first meeting the doctor, I arrived by myself for the first time at his office and was finally at peace with everything. I was a different person now or maybe just the person I was meant to be. I drove to the office alone and felt little need to check or ritualize. When the doctor came out to greet me, he smiled and said, "Where are your parents?"

I smiled back and said, "I came by myself, Doc. I don't need them. Well, not for this I don't."

"I knew you were getting closer to that point, and I'm glad you're finally here. Now, come in and have a seat."

I took a seat right near the phone that was sitting on a clear, white counter. I used to need my parents to make sure I didn't use it but now, well now, things were different.

"I owe you everything, Doctor."

"No, I just treated you the only way I knew how."

"How is that?"

"Hopefully with some compassion."

"You truly did."

"Please, Steve, tell me how you feel as opposed to when you first started coming here."

"A complete turnaround, Doc."

"Let me hear."

"I go out to eat with my parents, see movies with them."

"But are you able to do things alone?"

"I drove here, didn't I?"

"Are you scared of putting things in food or using the telephone?"

"No, on both counts."

"That's great. I'm so happy to hear this."

"Thank you."

"But, do you have any friends to do things with, Steve?"

"No."

"And have you spoken to your brothers?"

"I think some relationships are irreparable."

"I'm sorry to hear that."

"And I'm sorry that I know these things to be true."

"Do you think you can make new friends?"

"Possibly. My dad thinks I should start working somewhere and eventually move out."

"That's a lot."

"Yes, but he always had high hopes for me."

"Well, Steve, as they say in AA, one day at a time."

After he said that, instead of shaking the doctor's hands, I stood up and hugged him.

"Thank you, Doc."

"It's truly been a pleasure to see your transformation, Steve. Before you, I was starting to think that I couldn't help anyone anymore but then you walked into my life."

"Don't make me cry."

"Well, I still need to see you monthly, Steve, to monitor the medicine and see how you are doing."

"Yes, Doc."

"Now get out of here."

As I drove home, I realized that as I was now approaching mid-life, I was finally happy. However, so much time was lost that I could never get back. Time to find a girlfriend, make friends, or develop a career. I knew this fact, though: Life was rich. I was living with the two people in the world who made me happiest. Maybe I would find a career but at this point, taking care of my parents who had spent so much time caring for me was more than enough. They were getting older and now I was finally able to assist with shopping, driving them to their doctor's appointments, and most of all, providing them with the love that they both had sought for all these years and deeply deserved. Hell, I even shoveled the driveway during the past New York winter.

February 2006

I was starting to see things clearer though I still was questioning God.

I went out to Wendy's with my mother and asked, "Why would the same God who has allowed AIDS, war, tsunamis, and Columbine to occur, care enough to save me from the devil?"

"You know, Steve," she said, "when your dad was younger, he had similar questions. He couldn't find the answers in the Jewish faith. So, eventually, he saw a priest."

"And what did he find?"

"That no matter how many times you see a priest, you're still going to get sick eventually and die. Hurricanes will still arise. Wars still happen. People still can't find jobs. The body gets sick with cancer; the mind gets sick sometimes, too. God doesn't mind questions. He's given us the ability to think and reason."

"Does he allow the devil to take over our souls?"

"There is no devil, Steve," she said. "Keep telling that to yourself and things will get better."

April 2006

I kept telling myself what my mom had told me. I also kept taking my medication, and I was feeling better. However, I knew there was no devil and I couldn't or wouldn't hurt anyone. The new medication had changed my life.

A year later, while my father was shoveling his ice-ridden driveway during one of New York's harshest winters, his heart gave out. The doctors said it was just an isolated incident and nothing more. For me, that is just not a good enough explanation. Yes, I beat OCD but I believed I killed my dad in the process. I put him through so much hellish checking and ritualizing, that I instinctively knew I played a part in his death.

My mother sat me down after I learned of his death and commenced to speak with me.

"He loved you, Stevie," she stated emphatically.

"I know this but I can't help but bear some guilt for putting him through so much evil and destruction."

"He would not want you to bear any guilt so please forgive yourself and do what he wants."

"What is that?" I asked.

"You need to write his eulogy to deliver tomorrow."

"Why do you want me to do it?"

"He would go through a wall for you and you should be able to do the same."

"I loved him and I still do," I said.

"Then, get to work."

I spent the night trying to watch television and write the eulogy as well. At first, it was difficult but after a few minutes, my dad's life or what I knew of it was unfolding in front of me and being depicted in my writing notebook.

I was going to speak the truth about my dad, no matter how controversial, complicated, and stubborn he might have been. I wrote the eulogy and then fell asleep, embracing the peaceful darkness that surrounded me.

The Next Day

After my mother and rabbi introduced me, I rose and walked up to the podium to deliver my father's tribute. I'd be lying if I said it was a crowded funeral as my dad was not a popular man outside of his family. I commenced my speech and my mouth trembling slowly gave way to the words that I created the night before.

"It seems like I hardly knew you, Dad, since you tried to protect me from all the secrets and dangers of life that a child finds out about anyway, no matter how hard the father wants to protect his child from making the same mistakes as he did as a young man. My dad would die for me and in some ways, he did, but he understood an important lesson which is that blood is thicker than water. He was a man of few friends but loved his family and was wise enough to realize that family always comes first. I told my mom last night that though the autopsy report might not have shown it, I feel responsible for his death. I can't help it because I put him through so much pain for so many years that I believe it weakened his heart and soul. My father knew how sick I was for so long and endured the heavy toll of getting caught up in my rituals. So, why did my father, whom some medical professionals would call an enabler, involve himself with my rituals? The answer is nothing less than stunning and heroic. The answer is that he loved me and couldn't stand to see me in pain. Like many religious prophets, he sacrificed himself for my well-being. For I am the one standing up here today while he has now passed on. Maybe it should have been me that left the world and not my wonderful daddy. That is for everyone here today to decide. My father made that decision every day of his life and wanted it that way. He would protect me to no end and that is how I would like to remember him. My father suffered immensely from his own demons as a young man as well. He only informed me when I was of adult age that his childhood was brutal and abusive. However, he shielded this part of his life from me for so long in order to protect me. My dad and I both grappled with religion and whether we were living up to God's standards, or ironically, as Jews, whether we were adhering to Christ's desires. I am here to tell you that it does not matter whether you are a Jew, Christian, or Muslim. It's how you live that determines what kind of person you are and my daddy was a superb person. He was not a perfect man but he was a great person despite what many people who thought they knew him believed. But I can confidently say this because not only was I watching, but I think God was as well. So there are good and bad people of all religions but in the end, only love and compassion matter. And my dad had plenty of both. I want to repeat that my father loved me immensely and told me so often, not only in his words but in his actions. On my dad's refrigerator, he placed a magnet on it years ago that said, 'If I can't do great things, then I will do small things in a great way.' God, he was wrong because Dad did great things in larger-than-life ways. He touched me deep inside and for that, I am able to say what I have always struggled to say to him. I love you, Dad.

"I will share a short anecdote that says a lot about my dad. When we belonged to a temple with a stereotypical, rich, self-serving rabbi who kept petitioning for raises, my dad at a secret meeting of the brotherhood stood up and said we could have a more compassionate temple without this man. My father was not going to sell out like so many loyal friends of the rabbi who would soon retell his comments to the ugly rabbi. I later asked my dad why he did this, knowing that in a small town, he could become a pariah. He talked to me as a man though I was much younger then and explained that a man without principle and family was not a real man. So let's end with what we do know about Daddy, and that is that he loved me to no end and I know he's watching over me right now, smiling, hopefully finally proud of me.

"Everyone in my family knew how sick I was for so long and the toll it took on my father but I am glad that he saw me at the end of his life progress socially, intellectually, and in my career as well. My conscience is and always will be very heavy when I think of his death.

"I think at this time, I will tell a slightly comical story that exemplifies my dad's character and his love for me. When I was about 11 years old, I was playing basketball for a coach who hardly played me. My father came to every game and watched every minute, nonetheless. At the end of one of our team's many lopsided losses, my dad approached the overweight but arrogant coach and said, 'You're losing every game and my son is better than your friends' children. Why don't you put him in the game?'

"The coach replied that he noticed how my facial tics flared up while I was in the game and he did not want to subject me to future embarrassment.

"'What does he have to be embarrassed about?' my dad replied.

"'Well, I guess I would have been embarrassed,' the coach said.

"My dad looked the coach straight in the eye and said, 'Sir, my son is a beautiful, wonderful person, and if you or your snobbish friends from the temple can't see or understand that, then it is indeed you and them who should be embarrassed. My son is too good of a person to be around you. This will be his last game.'

"As my father walked me out of the gymnasium and into the parking lot, I was unable to tell him how much I appreciated his standing up for me, but my dad always made it a practice to stand up for those who couldn't do it themselves. He did a great thing that day and he did hundreds of great things for me during the course of his lifetime. It is largely because of his strength and my mom's dedication to caring for me that I am able to finally stand up, look the world in the eye and say, 'Let's fight.'

"We both grappled with religion and whether we were living up to God's standards or ironically, as Jews, whether we were living up to Christ's desires. I am here to tell you that it does not matter. Whether you are a Jew or a Christian, it doesn't matter. It's how you live that dictates what kind of a person you are. There are good Christians and Jews. There are also bad Jews and Christians but in the end, only love and warmth matter. My dad and I fought for so long for salvation, scared of heaven, and most of all hell. But I am here to tell you, regardless of what we believed, whether we sought counsel with a rabbi or a priest, only kindness matters."

As I tried to continue with the eulogy I wrote, I started to cry and then the sobbing got more intense. I could see in the sparse temple that held the family together, that my mom was not crying. *She loved him*, I thought, *but she wanted to be strong for me and the others that were there.* I also could see my two brothers sitting down together in the front, crying, not as hard as me, but still crying just the same. I wanted to talk to them but there was nothing left to say. I figured they were still angry at me and could not understand the bond between my father and I. Few people could understand true, unconditional love, but my dad and mom both showed me fortunately what it felt like to experience such compassion. Fortunately, it occurred before I had to say goodbye to my old man.

I knew my life had not gone as I or anyone intended it to go, but I was thankful that my dad was able to see me progress before he left. I also knew that as strong as my mom was, she would need me too in her remaining years to assist her with keeping the family intact. However, when I looked at my two brothers who were starting to cry harder and I saw that they had left their families back on the other side of the country, I couldn't help but think they still wanted distance from me. They still saw me as a monster. My parents never did see me in that light. Rather, they saw me as a troubled man who needed special attention, not fear.

My disease had taken so much from me, but I was determined to make peace with my brothers so that my mom would be happy. I stepped off the beam and went toward my mother and hugged her, whispering simultaneously in her ear that "everything will be all right." I then led her and me to the front aisle where my brothers were now standing.

"It's over," I said. "I think it's time for all of us to come home. I am not a monster."